BAS		CAN		HAD		
BEN		PIT		HCC		TAR
FRY	10/96	VAN	619 S	HUL		

WATERLOO, WATERLOO

By the same author:

Painting Water

WATERLOO, WATERLOO

TERESA WAUGH

HAMISH HAMILTON
LONDON

First published in Great Britain 1986
By Hamish Hamilton Ltd
Garden House 57–59 Long Acre London WC2E 9JZ

Copyright © 1986 by Teresa Waugh

British Library Cataloguing in Publication Data

Waugh, Theresa
    Waterloo, Waterloo.
    I. Title
    823′.914[F]   PR6073.A91/

    ISBN 0–241–11748–8

Typeset at The Spartan Press Ltd, Lymington, Hants
Printed in Great Britain by
St Edmundsbury Press, Bury St Edmunds, Suffolk

For my Mother

Chapter I

The SS *Ionia* sailed sedately between the vast walls of the Corinth Canal. Most of her passengers were crowded around the rails in the bows, all eager for the moment when the ship would burst into the Aegean Sea. Some cheerful boys waved at the passengers and spat at them as they passed under a flimsy-looking bridge which spanned the canal high above the liner.

Among those in the bows was Major Jack Bennett, a small, elderly man with a distinctly military bearing. He wore khaki shorts, a khaki shirt, socks and sandals. On his head he had a white linen sun-hat and around his neck hung his binoculars. He was listening intently to the blurred tones of an Oxford don which were being relayed by a loud-speaker over the deck. Major Bennett already knew a certain amount about the history of Corinth, but he was ever ready to learn more. After all, these chaps had spent their lives in research. They knew their stuff. They had plenty to teach him. So far the visiting lecturers had impressed him more than favourably. He would be interested to hear what they had to say about the excavations on Crete.

Major Bennett had been looking forward to this cruise for years. In fact ever since leaving the Army. He had always promised himself that when he finally retired he would give himself a big treat – a Greek cruise – something really worth waiting for and saving up for.

Never a brilliant soldier, despite a fascination for military history and an unbounded admiration for Napoleon, Jack Bennett had, none the less, enjoyed his long years of service to Crown and country. He joined the Army on leaving school at the age of eighteen, in 1927. He was lucky. He had seen the world – India (well, Pakistan now), the Far East, North Africa, Germany – though never Greece. And he'd enjoyed it all.

When he was in his mid-thirties, shortly after the war, he had

1

married the sister of a brother-officer. The union was childless but happy. After some fourteen years of marriage the first Mrs Bennett died prematurely of cancer. Jack's brother officers were really good to him at the time. It had been a dreadful business. He was stationed at Aldershot then.

At the age of fifty-five, Jack, who had never managed to rise above the rank of major in a Gunner regiment, was obliged to retire from the Army. He was sorry to go but looked around optimistically for another job. He was lucky enough to be taken on as bursar at a girls' private school. He never particularly enjoyed the job, but it provided an income for ten years or so while leaving him with plenty of time to indulge his passion for history.

At about the same time as he retired from the army Jack married his second wife. Peggy was some sixteen years younger than Jack. She was a glamorous divorcee with a teenage son. Jack was dazzled by her. She, flattered by the attentions of this gentlemanly, older man and, no doubt, looking for somewhere to hang her hat, gladly accepted his offer of marriage. Her first husband was a rotter – an absolute bounder – only interested in making money. He dealt in machine tools, neglected his wife and son and eventually ran off with his secretary. Jack felt that Peggy had indeed been badly treated.

A year after his marriage Jack became the proud father of a baby daughter, Josephine. Life held many surprises. Meanwhile Peggy's son had left school and home and gone to join the Navy.

The time eventually came for Jack to retire from the bursarship. He would not miss the job and he was looking forward to his long-promised Greek cruise. It was 1974 and after a winter of power cuts and Edward Heath's three-day week a trip abroad would be like a tonic. Of course there was a Labour government now and the Lord only knew what that meant for the future.

Peggy, too, was delighted by the prospect of the cruise – you could never get enough sunshine in England. Soon she was busy planning her wardrobe with care. She would need several new dinner dresses and a couple of bikinis. She still had an excellent figure, particularly for a woman of her age.

Jack seemed more interested in ancient history and in the route they would be taking. He spent every evening with his nose buried in a book or a map, reading about Thermopylae or Salamis. Josephine whined and said that she wanted to come too. This was, of course, out of the question. She could stay with Peggy's mother who would probably spoil her dreadfully.

The ship sailed from Venice, down the Adriatic and through the Gulf of Corinth to the glories of the ancient world beyond.

Jack was amazed by the magnificence of the Corinth Canal. He had seen some fine sights in his time and this certainly measured up to the best of them. What a treat it all was. Everything lived up to his expectations. Or surpassed them. Yesterday they had been at Delphi, the next port of call was Heraklion, and the voyage had only just begun.

An American in a checked shirt was leaning on the rail beside Jack. He half-turned and said, 'Well, Major, this is what we'd call in the States "one helluva goddamn trip." You guys in Europe certainly knew a thing or two.'

Jack had little time for the New World. He cast a withering glance in the American's direction and said coldly, 'It is most impressive.' He vaguely wondered what had happened to Peggy.

At that very moment Peggy was busy removing a paperback book and a bottle of Ambre Solaire from a chair on the deck. The chair was set at a perfect angle to catch the afternoon sun as the ship steered a south-eastern course towards Crete. Peggy had been unfortunate. By the time she came on deck that morning all the best chairs were occupied. It was most annoying. Quite honestly, though, people had no business to reserve chairs for the whole day. It was quite unfair. People really were very selfish. For the last few days Peggy had been watching an elderly, blue-haired woman who tirelessly employed the most devious tactics in order to ensure that she permanently had one of the best chairs on deck. Peggy thought she must be Jewish.

As far as Peggy could see there was nothing particularly remarkable about the Corinth Canal. She couldn't understand what all the fuss was about. There seemed to be a huge wall of

3

sandstone or limestone – or something – on either side of the ship. That was all very well – and of course it was very clever of them to have dug the canal and so forth – but personally, she would rather be in the open sea. She moved the sun-oil and the paperback book to an unoccupied chair at the other end of the deck and settled down in the comfort of her purloined chair. If people went away to admire the view or whatever, then it was their misfortune if other people took their seats.

Peggy began to leaf through the pages of a glossy magazine. Her attention was attracted to an article entitled 'Sex and the Older Woman'. She began to read with interest.

Half an hour later Peggy was fast asleep. She was awoken abruptly by a voice saying, 'Excuse me, please, but I think I left something on this chair.'

She opened her eyes. The blue-haired lady was standing in front of her, dressed in a turquoise towelling robe.

'I have seen nothing,' said Peggy rudely. 'I suggest you look elsewhere and I certainly hope you are not suggesting that I have taken your things. They would be of no use to me.'

The blue-haired lady looked down her nose at Peggy and moved away without another word.

Presently Jack appeared.

'Ah, there you are,' he said and suggested that they go inside for a cup of tea.

'You go, dear. I don't want to lose this seat. I've been to a great deal of trouble to get it. What have you been doing?'

'Admiring the canal and listening to the lecture,' he answered.

'How dull,' said Peggy and closed her eyes.

Jack gave her a thoughtful look, turned and set off to find a cup of tea. The tea on the boat was not particularly good, but never mind, it was nice to have something in the middle of the afternoon.

In the Telemachus lounge where tea was being served Jack met a retired solicitor and his wife. The three of them had already made friends in the bar the night before.

The Browns lived in Hertfordshire. He had retired a few years ago and it was not their first cruise. They had been twice before. Couldn't recommend these cruises more highly. For

4

one thing they were so beautifully organised. The Browns were thinking of going to Egypt next year. The Nile cruise, you know. Jack envied them. They were a pleasant couple, thoroughly interested in everything they saw. They never missed a lecture and had brought a rich assortment of guide books and history books with them. Mrs Brown had been advised to read the novels of Mary Renault. She had noticed that several people on board were reading them. Was Jack familiar with them?

Jack had heard that they were good but he didn't really care for historical novels – even the best.

'We like to read up about the places we are going to before we set out,' said Mrs Brown. 'But there is so much to learn. I sometimes feel very ignorant.' She sipped her pale grey tea.

'I must say I'm looking forward to Knossos tomorrow,' said Jack.

They chatted away. Jack confided in the Browns that he loved history and was particularly interested in military history. He had to admit that he really knew more about modern times. There were dreadful gaps where ancient history was concerned.

Mrs Brown wondered how he managed to remember it all. Her trouble was that she could read a book one day and by the following week she would have forgotten everything about it – even the author's name!

'I certainly don't remember everything I read,' said Jack humbly. 'Have another cup of tea.' He looked round. 'Oh, it's too late I'm afraid. They've taken it away.'

'What I always say,' said Mr Brown, 'is that you're never alone with a book.'

They all agreed.

'Does your wife share your interest in the past?' Mr Brown asked Jack.

'Oh no, I fear not. She's more interested in the present. But then it takes all sorts . . . . My wife is considerably younger than myself, as you must have realised. We have a little girl you know. Josephine. She's nine. Peggy is kept very busy with her.'

'Our little grandson is nine too!' exclaimed Mrs Brown.

5

'Yes, I suppose it may seem a trifle ridiculous, but Josephine is the light of our lives. It's wonderful to have a young person around one in later life. It keeps one up to the mark, you know.'

'Josephine – that's a pretty name,' said Mrs Brown. 'And so unusual these days too.'

'We called her after the Empress Josephine,' said Jack. 'Poor Josephine. She was so badly treated by Napoloen. That's one thing I can never really forgive him.'

Mr Brown agreed. But Mrs Brown wasn't at all sure how Napoloen had treated Josephine.

Later Jack joined Peggy in their cabin. She was already halfway through the lengthy process of changing for dinner.

'I'll sit on the bunk out of the way while you finish changing,' Jack said. He sat down tidily, picked up a book and began to read.

Peggy was leaning over the dressing-table, her neck stretched out, her face close to the looking-glass. She was applying a thick coat of blue eye-shadow. Beside her a Marlboro cigarette with a bright red lipstick mark on the filter was smoking in an ash-tray.

'I've really got quite brown already,' said Peggy.

Jack looked up.

'Would you mind putting that cigarette out,' he said. 'It's smelling rather unpleasant.'

Peggy clicked her tongue, picked up the cigarette and inhaled deeply before crushing it out carelessly so that it was still left smouldering.

Twenty minutes later she was ready for dinner.

'How do you think I look?' she asked Jack as she twisted her hips and admired herself in the looking-glass.

'Very nice, dear,' Jack replied without looking up from his book.

Peggy's dress was white and very tight. It was tied in a bow over one shoulder, leaving the other shoulder bare. She wore high-heeled white sandals.

'See you in the bar in about ten minutes,' she said as she swept out of the cabin.

Jack put down his book, folded his spectacles and put them neatly beside the book. He stood up, picked up the ash-tray

6

and meticulously flushed the offending contents down the lavatory in the adjoining shower-room. Then he changed into a clean shirt, grey flannel trousers and a white linen jacket. He wore a regimental tie which he carefully adjusted in front of the looking-glass.

In the bar Peggy was talking about the relative merits of Ambre Solaire and Bergasol. You had to be ever so careful to choose the sun cream that suited your skin.

Jack joined his wife and the conversation turned to tomorrow's outing to Knossos. Peggy was rather annoyed as she had wanted to have her hair done in the morning and had made an appointment without taking the tourist schedule into account. She would have to change it now, which was rather a nuisance because if she went to the hairdresser in the afternoon she wouldn't be able to sun-bathe.

The next day, at crack of dawn, Jack was on deck to see the *Ionia* come alongside. The island of Crete was magnificent, stretched out peacefully in the shining waters under the clear sky. Jack was really looking forward to the outing. Of course all this mythology was rather confusing. He preferred hard facts, but there would be some fascinating things to see. And, by Jove, he admired those archaeologist fellows with their devotion to detail and their endless patience. If he had his time again, he wouldn't mind going on a dig or two.

At ten o'clock the passengers came ashore. They were a curious bunch. Most of them had seen a little too much of the sun in the last few days. A few were young. Most of them not so young. They carried guide-books, sun-glasses, cameras, walking-sticks. One of them even had crutches. He was a wonderful fellow. Would never give in. All sorts and shapes of hat adorned their heads. For the most part they were sensibly shod. On the whole they were a cheerful, appreciative crowd although one or two complained about the inconvenience of having to keep climbing in and out of buses. It was all very well for the young and fit.

Someone said loudly: 'To be quite honest, if people can't manage a trip like this, then they shouldn't come.'

It was a long, hot morning. Peggy's feet ached.

'No wonder, dear,' said Jack, 'if you wear shoes like that.' He

7

was very comfortable in his sandals.

Peggy cheered up when the guide told the story of Pasiphae's passion for the white bull of Crete, and of how Pasiphae had hidden inside the effigy of a cow in order to attract the attention of the bull.

'What a naughty girl!' Peggy exclaimed with glee.

It was a relief to hear these entertaining little anecdotes, especially if, like Peggy, you found it difficult to sort out the difference between the Minoans, the Macedonians, the Persians and all the rest of them. It really was most confusing. Of course Jack was clever. He could cope with all that. But still, where did it get you in the end? It had happened such a long time ago.

Peggy was glad to get back to the boat. She had taken the precaution of leaving some things on one of the best placed chairs on the deck. She looked forward to a pleasant afternoon's sun-bathing. She would go to the hairdresser in the morning.

The days passed agreeably by. Both Jack and Peggy, in their different ways, were having the time of their lives. They visited the Turkish coast which Peggy found horribly dirty and Istanbul which she thought very over-rated. The sun shone mercilessly all the time. Peggy's stomach began to peel. Jack had warned her that it was foolish to expose her fair skin too suddenly to the sun. British people could not take it. He'd learned that in India if nowhere else. But this wasn't India. Peggy couldn't understand it. She had never suffered from sunburn before.

The last two days were spent in Athens. It was extremely hot. Peggy, finding herself in a capital city, saw fit to put on her highest heels.

'My dear, you will never manage to walk up the Acropolis in those,' Jack told her before they left the ship.

She was determined that in Athens she should be elegant. In the event one of her heels broke off and she had to spend most of the morning hobbling around in the greatest discomfort.

Whenever Peggy went ashore she bought a great many things. It was all so cheap. It went to her head. Her cabin was stuffed with dolls in national costume, baskets, jewels, scarves, dresses, sandals and plaster reproductions of the Temple of

8

Poseidon at Sounion. She had also bought some hysterical little plastic statues of Silenus in a state of sexual excitement. They would make her friends at home laugh.

Jack wondered how she would ever manage to pack all the rubbish she had bought. They were due to fly home from Athens.

On the last night of the cruise there was a gala dinner on board. Peggy wore her best dress. Jack wore his dinner jacket. After dinner, old and middle-aged alike bopped the night away. They had had a wonderful holiday.

When the morning came for their departure Peggy had somehow managed to squeeze almost everything into her suitcases. Jack would still have to take a couple of extra baskets as hand-luggage.

The whole party travelled by coach to Athens airport. Jack felt a twinge of regret as he left the *Ionia* for the last time. He would never be able to afford another holiday like it. He had seen undreamed-of sights – Ephesus – Istanbul – Knossos – Troy – whole avenues of history had been opened up for him. He would have a lot of reading to do when he got home. Of course Peggy had not appreciated the same things as he had. But over the years he had learned not to expect that of her. At least she had enjoyed herself in her own way.

Now they were going back to a new life. Work, for him, was over. He could peacefully devote his remaining years to his little daughter and his hobbies.

At first Peggy had been horrified by the thought of Jack's retirement. The future looked bleak until she hit on the idea of running a village post office. Jack wanted nothing to do with the post office or the shop but he saw that for Peggy who was, after all, still young, it might be a solution. She would be kept busy and would be seeing people all day which would prevent her from being lonely when Josephine was at school.

After looking around for a few months, the Bennetts had found a delightful village shop in the heart of Devon, near where Peggy's mother lived. Peggy was thrilled with it and the sale had gone through shortly before they left for Greece. As soon as they reached home they would have to start thinking about the move.

9

Jack struggled across the tarmac, laden like a pack-horse with Peggy's baskets. The July heat was stifling. Peggy, sun-tanned and confident, strode ahead of him towards the aeroplane. She felt the holiday had done her good.

Chapter II

The village of Chadcombe in South Devon lies in rolling countryside not many miles from Exeter. When the surrounding fields are ploughed in the autumn, the earth is seen to be a rich, rosy red. The locals are proud of the red earth which runs in a narrow strip from somewhere in the North of England down into the heart of the West Country. Some fifteen or sixteen hundred people live in Chadcombe and the outlying farms. Besides the farmers and a number of retired professional people – all Conservative voters – and their wives, there is a handful of university lecturers – among them a solitary member of the Workers' Revolutionary party – and a few, a very few, genuine West Country working people.

In the 'fifties a small council housing estate was built. The Manor House has been there since the end of the sixteenth century. Finally the village hall – a wooden hut with a tin roof – was added during the affluent 'sixties.

Halfway down the main village street there is a Victorian school which still survives under the permanent threat of closure. The church is fifteenth century; there is a quaint thatched pub and next to that a butcher's shop. Beyond the butcher's shop is a post-war rectory – the Old Rectory had been bought by some Londoners. The 'Post Office & General Stores' is also in the main street. It is a pleasant, square building with a stucco front and a slate roof.

When the Bennetts bought the village shop they found it very run-down. Peggy couldn't imagine how people could bear to live in such conditions. Really dirty people they must have been – with only an outside toilet. Mind you, they were old and had been there since the Ark.

When all was said and done, it was a busy move for the Bennetts. Peggy called in a firm from Exeter to build her a

11

fitted kitchen. She had always dreamed of a fitted kitchen. The whole house needed decorating and everything had to be done while the Post Office remained open and while Peggy took lessons from a Post Office clerk on how to deal with all those forms and pensions and what-not. She sometimes wondered if she would ever get the hang of them, what with one thing and another. It was all go. She never had a moment to sit down from morning till night – let alone to make a hairdressing appointment. She looked a perfect sight.

Jack Bennett looked forward to the building and decorating being finished, then he would be able to settle down and quietly concentrate on his own things. Meanwhile he did a bit of wall-papering and painting. He hung a few pictures and put up some shelves. He also began to tidy up the small garden behind the shop. It had been let go completely. Everything he did, he did with meticulous care, but he did not feel up to painting the front of the shop so that was left to the builders. Peggy chose to have the shop painted bright pink. Jack thought it was a shame. He would have preferred pale yellow.

It was spring before all the work was finished and Peggy was quite ready for another holiday! But it would be a long time before they could afford one. Jack had bought the shop in Peggy's name. It was much more sensible and would save a lot of trouble when he died. They lived off Jack's pension, some savings and whatever Peggy could make from the shop.

Jack wanted the very best for Josephine, and Peggy thought the local schools were too rough for her – she was a sensitive child – so she was sent away to a girls' boarding school. Jack thought that, as an only child, Josephine would be lonely at home. Peggy agreed and, besides, it wouldn't do for her to pick up a common accent. The school fees seemed exorbitant, but Jack was able to pay them as the result of an insurance scheme which he had taken out years ago and which had just come to maturity. So off Josephine went, all alone, at the age of ten, to school in the Home Counties.

Mrs Yeo, who kept the keys of the village hall, said, 'Our children aren't good enough for the likes of them.'

Mrs Yeo had two no-good boys who were always vandalising the telephone box. Their mother couldn't understand why her boys were blamed for everything. It wasn't fair the way they were picked on.

At the end of the Bennetts' garden there was an old garage. It had been filled with all kinds of junk when they arrived – broken garden tools, rotting cardboard boxes, piles of old newspapers and so forth. The cart-track which led along the side of the Post Office to the garage was completely grown over. It would be impossible to get a car down it now. Jack had noticed the garage the first time he and Peggy had looked at the shop with a view to buying. It would be ideal for his collection of model soldiers. He probably had as many as two thousand and he was certainly looking forward to collecting more. Several important regiments were still missing. He had not, for instance, got any Cameron Highlanders. And what would he do without the Cameron Highlanders when he deployed his troops for the Battle of Waterloo?

Peggy laughed at Jack's soldiers. Just toys, she called them. Of course they were toys, but how infinitely enjoyable. Jack had known men who collected electric trains. They were toys, too, and it was certainly no sillier to collect soldiers. Peggy was glad that he had the garage to put them in. She didn't want to dust them.

Josephine loved the soldiers. She longed to see them laid out in formation ready for battle. Perhaps Daddy would have them all ready to attack by the time she came back from school.

The Bennetts found their new neighbours friendly and helpful on the whole. Jack particularly enjoyed his visits to the pub. Before long he was recognized as a regular and welcomed into the group of old fogeys who gathered most evenings round the bar, and his new friends soon began to order a 'Major's special' with a knowing wink as soon as they heard his tread or saw his neat, military figure approaching.

It was good to make new friends at Jack's time of life, especially as many of his old friends had died or dispersed, and it was a pleasant walk down to the pretty little pub of an evening. Jack thought he might even get a dog one day. He would enjoy taking it for walks in the countryside. He had plenty to do at home, but it was nice to take a bit of exercise and a dog would certainly force him to do that.

13

When Josephine came back from school for the Easter holidays, she found that things had changed at home. To start with the builders had finished their work. The inside of the house looked like a home on a television advertisement. It was quite wonderful. When her parents first moved into Chadcombe, Josephine was bitterly disappointed. She thought it would all be such fun – having a shop. Instead, her mother shouted at her whenever she appeared behind the counter and the rest of the shop was in such a beastly mess with nowhere at all for Josephine to go and hide. She had imagined herself selling sweets all day, using the till with stylish efficiency, but her mother decided that she was too young for that and that she would almost certainly ring up the wrong sums.

Of course she wouldn't ring up the wrong sums. Why should she? Her mother was just being mean and probably enjoyed playing with the till herself which was jolly babyish.

By the time the Easter holidays came, Peggy had outgrown the novelty of the till so she began to allow Josephine to deal with simple transactions. Mind you, if Peggy found the till was out by so much as one penny by the end of the day, there would be real trouble.

Jack was glad to see his daughter back. He was always happy to talk to her and she enjoyed coming to the garage with him to admire his soldiers. While she was at school he had cleared out the garage, painted the doors and the window, installed a large trestle table for his campaigns and a gas heater to keep himself warm. He spent hours in the garage, making *papier mâché* hills and painting model soldiers and trees. By the beginning of the Easter holidays the Duke of Marlborough and Prince Eugene of Savoy were preparing to attack the French flanks at Malplaquet – of course you had to imagine a far bigger army – 'into a thousand parts divide one man' and so forth. Malplaquet was the first battle that Jack had laid out since coming to Chadcombe. He would leave it there for a week or two before beginning to work on another.

Mrs Yeo came into the village shop for her family allowance and a few odds and ends she'd run out of. She'd heard that Josephine had been home for several days. She hadn't seen her since Christmas. But Josephine was not in evidence.

14

'How's Josephine, then?' Mrs Yeo asked Peggy. The poor mite, she must miss her mummy when she was away at school. But still a good education was nice if you could afford it.

Josephine was in the garage playing with her father's soldiers.

Mrs Yeo told Mr Yeo at tea that Josephine was a queer child. If Mrs Yeo had a daughter she wouldn't want her to go playing with toy soldiers. It wasn't natural – not for a girl. Come to that the Major was a bit odd. Fancy a fully grown man shutting himself up in a garage all day with a lot of dolls. That's what they were when you came to think of it – dolls. She knew there was no accounting for tastes, but you would think he could find something better to do. Perhaps he was a bit simple. Mind you, they were a funny lot, the new people at the shop. Mrs Chedzoy, who cleaned for them, said that Mrs Bennett had been married before. She'd got a son in London or somewhere. No one here had ever seen him. Perhaps there was something strange about him too. Mrs Chedzoy said that Mrs Bennett could be quite rude at times. She had always been polite enough to Mrs Yeo, but then there hadn't been any call for unpleasantness. Anyway you couldn't really trust Mrs Chedzoy. Mrs Yeo had always thought she was a peculiar woman . . . .

Mr Yeo wondered how it felt for his wife to be the only sane person in the village.

It was supper time at the Post Office and Jack and Josephine were strolling back across the garden together. Josephine asked her father, for the hundredth time, to explain the allied campaign at Malplaquet. At supper she began to demand details of the casualties.

Peggy had heated up a ready-made steak and kidney pie and there were frozen peas and then vanilla ice cream for pudding. It was all very well for Jack and Josephine, they had nothing to do all day, either of them, they didn't have to leave her to get the supper all alone. Josephine could have at least laid the table.

Josephine's mind was still on Malplaquet and the dead. What did they do with all the bodies? Were there really thirty thousand dead and wounded? Who picked them all up? What if

15

an arm or a leg had been shot off, did they just leave it there –
on the ground?

Jack pointed out that the losses at some of Napoleon's battles
were even greater.

'Nearly fifty thousand were killed at the Battle of Eylau
alone,' he said.

'Did the bodies stink before they had time to bury them?'
Josephine wanted to know.

Peggy was furious. Some people were trying to eat their
supper. Josephine should try to think about nicer things. It was
quite revolting to keep thinking about dead bodies.

Josephine helped herself to some more vanilla ice cream.
Peggy lit a cigarette and puffed the smoke inconsiderately over
her daughter's plate.

After supper Jack said that he could see that Peggy was tired.
She should go and sit by the fire while he washed up. He could
bring her a cup of coffee. Josephine needn't help him, she was
on holiday. She could lend a hand another day. He tidied up
carefully and when he had finished, he folded the drying-up
cloth neatly. Then he took out his book and went to join his wife
who was watching the television with Josephine in the sitting-
room.

Peggy said that it was time Josephine went to bed. She had
had a long day.

Josephine, whose mind was still on the Battle of Malplaquet,
said good-night to her parents but instead of going to bed she
decided to visit the garage. She imagined that by now the
battle might have been fought. Her father's soldiers would be
scattered, dead and wounded, over the whole surface of the
trestle table.

She tip-toed into the kitchen and out through the back door
into the garden. For a moment she was afraid that her parents
might have heard the door shutting. She paused to listen. The
noise of the television was very loud. Her mother was
engrossed in a comedy and couldn't possibly hear anything
else.

Josephine began to feel her way up the stone steps that led to
the lawn from the area outside the back door. She thought of
going back and turning on the light. The gleam from the

16

kitchen window would help her to see. But that would be dangerous and she did not want to risk being caught. Slowly she scrambled on up through the garden which rose steeply into the hill behind the house. She tripped, fell and nearly screamed as her hand encountered something cold and fat and dank. She moved and heard the fat thing move. She felt frightened and rather sick. She knew there were toads in the garden. She had seen them, stared at them in horror, when she first came to Chadcombe last summer. But she had never wanted to touch one.

At school she told another girl that there were toads in her parents' garden.

'So what?' the girl had asked.

'Once I picked one up,' Josephine had lied.

'Anyone can pick up a toad,' the girl had said. 'They're not scarey.'

Josephine thought, as she crept up the garden, that toads were jolly scarey. But now she had gone so far there was no question of going back to the house without having reached the garage.

Something rustled among the shrubs. Josephine held her breath. She was nearly there. She could make out the dark shape of the garage, just beyond the lilac. A few moments later she was there. She turned the door-knob. To her amazement and bitter disappointment the garage was locked. Hot tears of rage welled up in her eyes. How dare they! She stood still for a moment, lost in thought. She wondered if she would be able to see anything if she peered through the window. She imagined the army of tiny soldiers charging mercilessly across the battlefield, eager to kill and be killed.

The window was just beyond her reach but she supposed that if she could climb on the old tree stump beside the garage, catch onto the guttering and hang there, she might be able to look through it to the excitement beyond. She was glad when the moon came out from behind a cloud. The whole thing was too easy. In no time she had caught hold of the gutter, but she soon realised that she would have to work her way along it before she could look through the window. She swung from side to side, edging herself gradually along the guttering. Her hands hurt and her arms ached, but she was nearly there. She paused for a moment to rest. It was then that she felt the guttering give way. The noise shattered the quiet of the night, she fell, bounced off the tree stump and landed with a heavy thud on her back in the grass. A length of guttering crashed across her face.

Josephine felt a searing pain burn through her shoulder. It had all happened so quickly. Her first thought was for the broken gutter. Her parents would be furious; she must get away before she was caught. She tried to stand up but discovered that she was too weak. She passed out. When she came to she was damp and cold and in pain. It had begun to rain. Josephine started to cry. She wondered how long she would have to lie there until she was found. She was alone and lonely – utterly lonely – more lonely than she had ever been in her life, even at school. She supposed that the wounded must have felt like this on the battlefield after Malplaquet. She imagined herself surrounded on all sides by the dead and the dying. It was rather exciting in a way. She wondered if her body would start to rot before they came to get her. Then she lost all sense of time.

In the morning Jack brought Peggy her tea in bed. With it there was a postcard from a friend in Malta.

'It's all right for some,' said Peggy.

On her way downstairs to prepare the breakfast, Peggy banged on Josephine's door.

'Time to get up,' she shouted.

Half an hour later she was sitting at the kitchen table with Jack. He had eaten his boiled egg. She had eaten two crispbreads. She lit a cigarette and poured herself another cup of tea. She thought Jack ought to go and tell Josephine to get up. In her day children had never been allowed to lie in bed all morning. Jack suggested that Josephine might be tired. After all she probably had to get up early at school and she was only young.

Peggy thought Jack spoiled Josephine – and there was nothing more unattractive than a spoilt child. Josephine should come down and have her breakfast. It was nearly nine o'clock. Time to open the shop. Mrs Chedzoy would be here in a minute. Peggy had a lot to do. So had Mrs Chedzoy. Josephine could at least wash up the breakfast.

Jack said he would have another cup of tea and finish the article he was reading in the *Daily Telegraph* before waking his daughter. Peggy turned to the woman's page of the *Daily Express*. At nine o'clock she went to open the shop. Jack went upstairs to wake Josephine. He knocked quietly on her door. He didn't want to waken her harshly. There was no answer, so he turned the handle slowly, gently pushed open the door and tip-toed into the room and over to the bed. As he bent down to kiss his daughter, he was amazed to see that the bed was not only empty, but that it had been made.

'Got up already?' said Peggy. 'How peculiar. I didn't hear her.'

They searched the house and the shop. She couldn't have gone out because all the doors were still locked on the inside.

Jack began to panic.

'I think I'll just have a look in the garden,' he said.

'She can't be in the garden. Silly child, she must be hiding – in the cupboard or under the bed – or somewhere. Leave her. She'll turn up. I've got things to do in the shop. You can clear up the breakfast. If she behaves like this she can do without breakfast. It'll serve her right. I've no time . . . .'

Jack didn't hear the rest, he had unlocked the back door and was halfway up the steps to the garden.

He hurried across the grass towards the garage, and suddenly saw her. She was lying quite still on her back. Her face was white, her hair and clothes drenched. She looked almost like someone wounded in battle. Across her small body, looking like some horrible weapon, lay a piece of broken guttering. He hurried towards her and knelt beside her. To his immense relief she was breathing.

19

Chapter III

Peggy sometimes wondered if her son, Nigel, was quite like other men. He had never, so far as she could remember, ever brought a girl home.

In fact Peggy hardly ever saw Nigel who, having left the Navy after a few years without a commission, now lived in a bed-sitter in London and worked in the linen department of a large West End store. Peggy was not particularly proud of him.

The Bennetts had been at Chadcombe for some nine months before Nigel rang to say that he was due for a week's holiday and that he would like to come down and see them.

It wasn't a very convenient moment from Peggy's point of view. Josephine was in hospital. She had had an accident. No, nothing serious. In fact she had brought the whole thing upon herself – the silly child – and caused her parents a great deal of trouble. Well, Nigel could come if he wanted, but he needn't think his mother would have much time to spare. He couldn't expect her to spend all day running around behind him. Yes, Jack was all right. Not that she saw much of him these days. When he wasn't visiting the hospital he spent most of his time shut up in the garage with those silly toys of his.

Peggy put down the telephone and returned to the shop where a selection of jams was waiting to be put on the shelf. It was all very well for Jack – he had nothing to do all day. You would think he might help her sometimes. He might even be glad of her company. It must be lonely in that shed. Peggy felt thoroughly cross. No one could suppose she enjoyed putting jam pots on shelves. She had hardly seen a soul all morning – only Mrs Little who'd been in for her pension book which she'd left behind last week and a few children buying sweets on the way to school. And now Nigel was coming. He would be just as likely to get under her feet.

The shop door opened and Mrs Yeo came in.

Mrs Yeo asked after Josephine. The poor little dear – it was a mercy she hadn't broken her back.

At the sight of Mrs Yeo, Peggy brightened. Mrs Yeo was always full of news. She knew everything that happened in the village and was only too happy to share her knowledge. Peggy was highly entertained by all the scandals and dramas that took place. Life was stranger than fiction.

Half an hour later Mrs Yeo was still there. She was shopping for her neighbour who was having a baby in the change and whose youngest was fifteen. The poor woman was so embarrassed she hadn't dared to put her nose outside her house for the last five months. Well that was silly really when you came to think of it. After all everyone would have to know in the end.

Jack came into the shop briefly to announce that he was just off to hospital. He was carrying a shopping basket and wondered if there was anything Peggy needed. He was going to buy a few grapes on the way, and some sweets. He already had a book in the basket. An illustrated history of British regiments. It would give Josephine something to take her mind off things.

Mrs Yeo thought the Major was definitely queer.

'Fancy giving a little girl a great long book about soldiers,' she said to Mr Yeo that evening. 'You'd hardly think she'd be wanting books anyway. Not at her age.'

Jack drove slowly to Exeter. He was thinking of Jena. One of Napoleon's greatest victories and he had never yet laid it out. It might be something to do to amuse Josephine when she came out of hospital. She would soon be home now and she would enjoy that. The doctor only wanted to keep her under observation for a couple more days. She had broken her collar bone, but apart from that there didn't seem to be anything the matter. Of course she was bound to be suffering from shock, but she would soon get over that. It was a shame that Peggy couldn't – or wouldn't – spare that little bit of extra time to visit Josephine in hospital. There was no doubt about it, the child could do with more attention from her mother. Peggy's attitude to Josephine sometimes made Jack sad.

Josephine was delighted when she saw her father appear with his shopping basket. She wondered what he had brought her today.

'Here comes Daddy,' said a young nurse brightly as she bustled busily by.

Josephine scowled at the nurse. It was nothing to do with that nosey nurse. Josephine sometimes like to pretend to herself that outsiders mistook Jack for her grandfather. It was so embarrassing him being old.

Jack brought fruit and sweets and books and comics out of his basket. He told Josephine that on his way in he had seen the doctor who said that she would be allowed home tomorrow.

'I want Mummy to come and fetch me,' she said harshly. That silly nurse had quite spoiled her pleasure.

'It will probably be me because Mummy's so busy with the shop.'

Josephine looked sulky.

Jack supposed that the child disliked hospital. That would account for her bad temper. But she cheered up when he told her about his plans for the Battle of Jena. He would probably need a few more Prussians, but they could work on that at home. He hoped he wasn't running out of paint. Josephine begged to be allowed to go back to school a few days late. Then she would have more time to help her father with the battle.

That evening at supper Peggy was feeling particularly irritable. How was she ever supposed to find time to get her hair done? She thought the hospital was behaving in a very irresponsible way by allowing Josephine out so soon. She was sure it would be far better to keep her in for a couple more days.

'Aren't you looking forward to having her back?' Jack asked.

Of course she was. But all the same, you had to put the child's health first. What if anything went wrong when she got home? And then there was Nigel. Peggy had forgotten to tell Jack that Nigel would be coming down for a week on Saturday. So inconsiderate, Nigel. He might have asked Peggy if it suited her – his coming like that – out of the blue. He hadn't given his mother a thought in months and then, just because it was convenient for him, he announced he was going to stay for a week. In Peggy's opinion the young were very selfish.

Jack thought it would be nice to see Nigel and to hear all his London news. It would make a change and might cheer Josephine up.

The only change Peggy wanted at the moment was a visit to the hairdresser.

Jack said her hair looked very nice to him.

She was perfectly furious. It didn't look at all nice. Couldn't he see the roots. They were beginning to show black. Of course it was quite obvious that he never looked at her any more, or he would have noticed how badly she needed a rinse. She supposed he didn't mind having a wife who always looked a mess. She who was used to taking such good care of herself. What would Nigel think when he arrived? He would be appalled to think his mother was neglecting herself.

'Well, dear, Thursday's early closing day. You make an appointment for Thursday and I'll look after Josephine.'

Peggy certainly couldn't wait till Thursday. She had made an appointment for the morning. Jack would have not to be selfish for once. The toy soldiers could do without him while he minded the shop for a few hours. If anyone wanted anything complicated from the Post Office, they would have to come back later.

What about Josephine?

Josephine could stay in hospital until after lunch. It wouldn't hurt her. She couldn't expect everything to revolve around her.

Jack helped himself to a second spoonful of vanilla ice-cream. They seemed to be having ice-cream rather often lately. He thought it would be wisest to make no comment at the moment, however. A hint of criticism might not be too well received.

The next morning, while Peggy was having her hair done, Jack looked after the shop. He also prepared lunch for Peggy's return. He laid the table neatly and even put three or four daffodils in a glass in the middle. He made a fish pie from a packet of frozen cod and a packet of Smash. He opened a tin of carrots which he left ready to be heated on the oven. He also opened a tinned sponge pudding and made some custard from a packet.

Poor Peggy, he could understand how things sometimes seemed to be too much for her. He felt it was partly his fault. After all she was still a young woman – and a good-looking one at that. She deserved to have a bit of a good time – to go out a little. She needed caring for.

Peggy was back by one o'clock, her hair a new gleaming shade of gold. She took a looking glass from her bag and peered into it, tweaking at the occasional glossy curl. Her long nails shimmered with a new frosted nail varnish called 'Ice Maiden'. Her trip to the hairdresser's had done her the world of good.

'Did you have a busy morning then, dear?' she asked.

'Not too bad. I managed all right. A couple of people wanted stamps. Nothing else from the Post Office. By the way, you're out of toilet rolls.' Mrs Willoughby from the Manor House had wanted toilet rolls, but Jack hadn't been able to find any.

A ripple of discontent appeared on the surface of Peggy's good humour.

'Of course we have toilet rolls. You just didn't look properly. You can never find anything.' She bustled around the shop, pulling things irritably off shelves. There appeared to be no toilet rolls. Mrs Willoughby was a good customer and Peggy felt piqued at not having been able to provide her with what she wanted. What would she think of Peggy? Peggy was also annoyed at having missed Mrs Willoughby herself. The whole thing was particularly irritating.

'Don't worry about the toilet rolls now, dear. Come and have lunch,' said Jack.

Peggy was gratified to see the lunch laid out and so she regained her good humour. It was really quite sweet of Jack to have put the daffodils on the table. The old fusspot. She tucked into her fish pie and carrots. But no thank you, she wouldn't have any sponge pudding and custard.

Jack urged her to have just a little.

Didn't he realise that she had to think about her figure? Nothing was more fattening than sponge pudding. The thought might have occurred to him. Well, he'd just have to eat it up himself. Peggy lit a cigarette.

24

That afternoon Jack fetched Josephine from hospital. He was really looking forward to the morning when he would be able to get back to his soldiers and Jena. But when the morning came Peggy sent him off to the cash-and-carry for toilet rolls.

'Get green ones, dear,' she said. 'Mrs Willoughby has a green bathroom *en suite*.'

Jack wondered how on earth Peggy knew what colour Mrs Willoughby had painted her bathroom.

Mrs Wescott used to work up at the Manor House and she had told Peggy all about it.

When Jack left for the cash-and-carry Peggy made herself a cup of coffee and lit a cigarette. She sat in the kitchen waiting for the sound of the bell from the front door of the shop. She longed for company and was tickled to death to hear of all the goings-on in the village. She looked at her watch. It was half past ten. No one had been into the shop yet this morning and Mrs Chedzoy didn't come to clean on Thursdays. She spread the *Daily Express* out in front of her and read about a company director's wife in a love tangle in Wimbledon. She gazed out of the window at the bank which rose steeply up to the garden. It was raining. She glanced back at the paper and mused for a moment about the company director's wife. It was a shame really that she and Jack lived in the back of beyond. What chance had she, Peggy, of a love tangle – here – in the middle of Devon? Just because Jack was a hundred years old he felt he could treat her like an old woman too. Didn't he realise that she was still young and good-looking? Men were so self-centred. She hoped Jack would remember that the toilet rolls had to be green. That was the least he could do.

This company director's wife was a couple of years older than Peggy. Peggy squinted at the photograph in the paper. She, Peggy, looked much younger and was altogether better-looking. It wasn't fair. If she lived in Wimbledon she could be involved in any number of love tangles. Peggy did not care to dwell on the fact that she had just turned fifty. In any case, it was hardly a woman's age that counted. It was her attitude of mind. Besides, some women of fifty were far more attractive than others of thirty – and looked younger too. Peggy had kept her figure nicely. Many men preferred more mature women.

25

Josephine came into the kitchen and complained about having to go back to school with her arm in plaster. It wasn't fair.

'Life is not fair,' said Peggy sharply. 'Now run along, dear, and find something to do.'

Josephine slammed the kitchen door. Peggy glanced back at the paper and turned the page. There was a story about a pop star and a Swedish actress. Without a doubt, some people had all the luck! Well, of course, she didn't expect to move in a world of pop stars and actresses, but she could do with a bit more fun than she was getting at the moment. The truth of the matter was that she had been born at the wrong time. Of that she was certain. Her life would have been completely different if she had been ten years younger. She had more or less missed out on the 'sixties. She felt a twinge of almost unbearable jealousy.

Suddenly Peggy heard the shop door. She jumped up excitedly and hurried through to the Post Office just in time to see Mrs Yeo's younger boy pocketing a Milky Way.

It was too much. How could she be expected to run a shop with types like him about?

The boy was quite brazen. His mum said he could have a Milky Way if he ran down the shop for her fags.

Peggy marked the cigarettes and the chocolate bar down in Mrs Yeo's book and wondered sourly what the world was coming to.

Things cheered up a little when the pharmaceuticals rep. called. He was a young man and nice-looking. Yes, he had a moment to stop off for a cup of coffee, and was much obliged.

When Jack came back, his arms laden with green toilet rolls, Peggy was ensconced in the kitchen with the pharmaceutical man. They were on their third cup of coffee and she was laughing extravagantly at everything he said. He was a one.

Jack had the impression that he was somehow interrupting. In his confusion he dropped the toilet rolls.

Well, the rep. had to be getting along. He would be back next month. Ever such a nice cup of coffee. Jolly good show. He sidled quickly out of the kitchen while the Major, looking bloody ridiculous with his backside in the air, delved under the

26

table for toilet rolls. The rep. winked at Peggy and was gone. Funny a good-looking woman like that being married to such an old stick. Attractive woman too . . . a little old for him though . . . .

When Jack had retrieved the toilet rolls, he called Josephine and with a sense of relief made his way with her to the garage. They had matters to discuss.

Peggy looked around helplessly. What should she do now? Jack had chased away the rep. It was too early for lunch and there was no one in the shop. Soon Nigel would be arriving. She realised that after all she was quite looking forward to seeing him. He would provide a diversion. Things might be rather different with him around. He might even be good company. It was no use relying on Jack or Josephine for company. They were both too concerned with toy soldiers.

In the garage Jack was explaining Napoleon's tactics at Jena to Josephine. This was the first chance he had had to talk to her since she came out of hospital. He and Josephine were quite happy together. Well, he was happy and he would be very much mistaken if she weren't happy too.

The result of Jena, according to Jack, was inevitable – a foregone conclusion. Prussian tactics were far less advanced than those of Napoleon and his Grand Army. The Prussian generals were all old men. Jack's right hand was placed inside the front of his jacket as he spoke.

'And you see, Josephine, the Prussians might have fared better if they had waited for the support of the Russians. They failed to do so and as a result their army was routed – routed.'

Josephine looked up at her father with wide eyes. She wondered how he knew so much. He went on and on talking, pacing up and down as he did so. Sometimes she stopped listening. It was all so complicated. But she knew her father was excited by the prospect of laying out this new battle. They needed a wood and a village. Josephine just wished they could stop talking and get on with the fun.

Chapter IV

Nigel caught the Golden Hind from Paddington. He was glad to be getting out of London for a few days. Not that he didn't enjoy his job. There were some good quality linens about these days and the department was always busy. There was never a dull moment. But lately he had been increasingly bothered by the persistence of his girl friend Suzanne. Suzanne was a nice girl, but she would pester him so. He enjoyed going to the cinema with her on Saturday nights, and they had even been to the zoo together once, but visits to her parents' home in Cricklewood for Sunday dinner were beginning to upset him. He suspected that both Suzanne and her mother might expect more from him than the friendship he was prepared to offer.

Although Nigel was nearly thirty, he had no intention of getting married yet. He wasn't really sure that marriage would ever be for him. For one thing, the idea of permanently sharing a bed with another person made him feel slightly sick. He couldn't bear the idea of an alien body turning and sweating and bumping into him – coughing and snoring and heaven knew what. He had heard people talk of keeping each other's feet warm in bed. The idea positively revolted him.

When he was in the Navy, Nigel had been made to feel that he wasn't quite like the other lads. He had once been dragged by his mates, under conditions which he preferred to forget, and with results which he preferred to forget, to a squalid room in a back street of Singapore. Never mind. Those were long ago days now. But the situation with Suzanne was becoming decidedly awkward. He would have time to think the matter over while he was on holiday. He didn't want to have to stop seeing Suzanne. No, not really. She was company and she was quiet and kind. But he did object to her linking arms with him as though he belonged to her. Neither did he care for the way she had of getting him alone and then standing uncomfortably close. It even made him feel slightly frightened. He had not thought Suzanne was like that. She had seemed such a shy girl when he had first met her in the record department. Perhaps all women were the same. Which did not mean that he need be as weak as most men. It was Nigel's considered opinion that most men were trapped into marriage. There could be no other explanation for their relinquishing their freedom the way they did.

Nigel hadn't seen his mother for a long time. His thoughts turned to her and Jack. There was another man who had been trapped into marriage. He wondered what had taken Jack and Peggy to Devon. It could hardly have been the proximity of Peggy's mother. Peggy had never been able to get on with her mother. Nigel imagined Peggy feeling a bit cut off down there in the West Country.

The train sped through Tiverton Junction. Nigel looked at his watch. Only a few more minutes. Exeter was the next stop. He stood up and took his mackintosh down from the rack, he tucked the paperback Western he had bought for the journey into the pocket. He was the sort of person who liked to be ready by the door when the train stopped. It would be most inconvenient to be carried on to Newton Abbot. The train stopped outside Exeter for some ten minutes. Nigel wished he had not stood up so soon. But it was too late to go back to his seat now. Other people were blocking the corridor.

Jack was at the station to meet him. Nigel thought his stepfather looked rather older than when he had last seen him.

Chadcombe seemed like abroad to Nigel. Jack and Peggy must find it very dull all the year round. The weekend passed slowly and Nigel wished he had stayed in London. He missed work and it occurred to him that he even missed Suzanne. Suzanne didn't complain as much as either Peggy or Josephine – or so it seemed to him.

Peggy planned to make use of her son to mind the shop. After all he worked in a grand enough department store – he ought to be an expert by now. He could hardly mind giving her a chance to get out and about a bit.

Jack found that he didn't really have all that much to say to

Nigel. Not that Nigel was a bad boy, but he must be a bit of a disappointment to his mother – not getting a commission and so forth. Jack couldn't really understand a chap not getting a commission. A bit soft, he called it. And of course a job in a shop selling sheets wasn't ideal. But then you had to face up to the fact that jobs were hard to come by these days. Still, it was a bit of a shame when you came to think of it. Not a very manly job. On the other hand Nigel had never caused his mother any trouble. A quiet, polite boy. Of course that father of his hadn't been any help. Jack felt that a boy definitely needed a father. He himself had fond memories of his own father, now long since dead.

On Tuesday afternoon Nigel went off to Exeter on the bus. He didn't think he could stand being stuck out in the country any longer. Not that he put it quite like that to Peggy. He told her that he was going to have a look at the cathedral.

Peggy was furious. You'd think Nigel would want to spend some time with his mother. It wasn't as if he had a chance to see her very often. He could have helped her to put away the frozen goods that had just been delivered. The deep freeze in the shop really needed clearing out.

When Mrs Willoughby came in Peggy was busy counting packets of fish fingers. But she quickly dropped the fish fingers and hurried to help Mrs Willoughby, offering her green toilet rolls and a new brand of artificial cream which was gorgeous for cakes. Mrs Willoughby wanted neither. She had just run out of bacon. Peggy had one packet left but she'd sold it that morning. How most unfortunate. She'd have some more tomorow. Her son was staying and he'd been eating her out of house and home. Would Mrs Willoughby believe it? Mind you, it was good to see a boy with a healthy appetite.

Mrs Willoughby agreed. Her own sons ate like horses.

Peggy had seen the Willoughby boys. They had been into the shop from time to time. Ever so nice-looking – both of them. The two women went on to discuss the weather. Then Cynthia Willoughby had to be on her way. She secretly wished she could think of something else to say. She didn't particularly like Mrs Bennett but there was no one at home and one occasionally felt the need for another human being. She had come to hate the silence of an empty house and at the moment both her sons were away, staying with friends, and her husband, Henry, was out at a meeting and wouldn't be back till late. Her married daughter lived in London.

Cynthia walked back through the village with her golden retriever, Lollipop, at her heels. Lollipop was old, obese, half-blind, rheumaticky and smelly, but at least she was a companion. Cynthia would never agree to having Lollipop put down. Her husband had been telling her for months that she was only being selfish, but as long as the dog was happy she could see no reason to destroy it. Lollipop went everywhere with Cynthia who, years ago now, had had bars put in the back of her car to prevent the young puppy from jumping out of the boot into the back seat. Poor old Lollipop, she wasn't capable of that any longer.

As she turned into the drive, Cynthia saw a strange young man walking up the village street. Funny, she thought. I don't think I've seen him around here before. She gave him a second look. He was small, thin, pale and bespectacled. He wore a grey flannel suit and highly polished black shoes – like school shoes – and carried a mackintosh over his arm. Rather out of place in a country village.

Cynthia walked on up the drive to the house. She was looking forward to the boys coming home. But they'd only be back a few days before they were off again – one to Oxford and the other to Eton. She was glad and surprised when she saw Henry's car parked in front of the house but she was disappointed a few minutes later when he told her that he had to go out again.

'Where did you go?' he asked.

'Oh, just down to the shop. That silly woman is dreadfully inefficient, you know. She's always run out of everything. It's most annoying. Last time I went in she had no lavatory paper and today she had mountains of frightful green lavatory paper and no bacon.'

Henry said he was late and had to be going.

'Come on Lollipop,' said Cynthia, 'let's go and pick daffodils.' The dog loped off behind her.

Until a few years ago Cynthia's passion had been for hunting, but she had hurt her back in a bad fall and could no longer ride. She tried not to complain but life was no longer the same.

The thin young man Cynthia had passed at the gate walked on towards the shop. Nigel had enjoyed his trip to Exeter but he felt slightly nervous as he walked back through the village. He wondered who the nice-looking lady with the dog was. She had stared at him rather rudely, he thought.

When Nigel reached the shop he found his mother with a cigarette hanging out of the corner of her mouth. She was dusting shelves and dropping ash everywhere.

'Ah, there you are,' she said. 'Just lock the door behind you and pull the blind down. It must be five o'clock.'

She went on to tell him that Mrs Willoughby from the Manor House had been in. Such a nice person. A real lady – and you should see her sons. Such well-mannered boys. Properly brought up in an old-fashioned way. Not enough of that around these days. Good-looking boys they were too.

Nigel decided to go and find Jack in the garage. He found his stepfather's soldiers rather amusing. More fun than his mother's endless chatter. Jack was mixing pieces of newspaper in a bucket of water. *Papier mâché.* Josephine, who was with her father, was tearing up old papers. She was having a certain amount of difficulty because of her plaster.

'We need a hill or two for our battlefield,' Jack explained.

Nigel didn't know much about Napoleon's battles. He asked about Jena.

Jack was delighted to explain. Nigel was a polite boy, and very helpful. He didn't get under anybody's feet and he seemed pretty interested in the battle of Jena. It was a pity Peggy couldn't appreciate the fun they were all having. The thought of Napoleon as a young general writing to the faithless Josephine from Italy flashed across his mind. Many years ago Jack had come to the conclusion that a man could never really count on a woman. Women were never satisfied with their lot. Besides men and women had different aims, they thought differently, they argued differently and they felt differently. When you thought you'd at last understood their point of view, they always managed to think up something else to confuse the issue. Never the twain should meet, there were no two ways

32

about it. At the moment Josephine was a joy and a happy companion, but Jack assumed that she would eventually go the same way. But he didn't think she would ever be quite like her mother. She was a clever girl.

The walls of Jack's garage were papered with plans of military campaigns, all drawn up in pen and ink and with the utmost precision by Jack himself. Nigel was fascinated by them. He vaguely wondered what his mother and stepfather had in common. They were both involved in different things and apparently uninterested in whatever the other was doing. Perhaps they only stayed together for financial reasons – it could hardly be for companionship.

Nigel wasn't sure what he thought of companionship. You could feel more alone with someone else than by yourself sometimes. He thought of Suzanne. A life of companionship with Suzanne. He would lose all his privacy. She was probably one of those women who could read your thoughts. Then he thought of all that sweating in bed – oh no. He had been perfectly happy wandering around Exeter alone that afternoon. He and Jack might go to the pub together presently. What need was there for a permanent companion? After all you saw people at work every day – you could hardly want them with you all night as well.

'When I've finished what I'm doing we might take a walk to the pub,' Jack suggested. He was pleased to see how closely Nigel was inspecting his plans of Marlborough's march on the Danube. Nigel was more intelligent than Jack had thought. Surprising he never got a commission when you came to think about it.

Later Jack and Nigel set out for the pub, leaving Josephine watching the television. Josephine hated Nigel. What business had he to turn up here just because he felt like it? Her mother didn't seem very interested in him and as for Josephine, she wouldn't mind if she never saw him again. He never addressed a word to her. And how dare he come into the garage! The garage belonged to her father and she was the only other person who was supposed to go there. And she didn't see why her father had to go to the pub with Nigel.

'Has Nigel got a girlfriend?' she asked her mother who was

33

watching the regional news with her.

'Sh-sh, dear,' said Peggy. She was interested in a case of indecent exposure in Exeter. The fourth case in the last month. This time two girls had been able to give the police a clear description of the man they were looking for.

'It's perfectly disgusting!' Peggy was truly indignant. 'What sort of a man would go around doing that? One wonders what kind of a background he must come from. Very lower class I should think. It seems that he's quite a young man too.' Peggy knew what she would do with offenders of his type – cut it off!

'Cut what off?' asked Josephine.

'Nothing dear, you wouldn't understand.'

When the men came back from the pub they were hungry for supper.

Peggy thought Nigel looked a bit flushed in the face. He was more talkative than usual. It was all very well for them. Had it ever crossed their minds to invite her to go along with them for a drink? Oh no. And she'd been working hard all day. Unlike some. Well they would just have to wait a bit for their supper. They could hardly expect Josephine to help – poor child – with her arm all in plaster.

Eventually they sat down to some rather dry baked eggs, some processed cheese and more vanilla ice cream.

Josephine was due to go back to school in a day or two. She lay in bed that night wondering how much she was dreading it. Home wasn't that much fun either. Her mother was always in a bad mood and her father seemed to be more interested in Nigel these days. Jena would never be ready now. She would probably have to wait until next holidays before she saw it. It was unfair. But school was vile too. The other girls were all horrid. They laughed at her and teased her when she got good marks which she usually did. They all had much nicer things than she did. Writing cases and expensive fountain pens and pretty pyjamas. Peggy said they were poor but Josephine didn't believe her. They couldn't be poor and have a shop. She wished she had the same things as the other girls and then they would probably like her. Life was miserable whichever way you looked at it. Her plaster made it impossible to find a comfortable position and she couldn't sleep. She thought of the night she had her accident. She wouldn't try anything like that again but she longed to go and play with those soldiers. Suppose they really did come to life after dark. She imagined being part of an infantry charge, running across uneven ground, her bayonet at the ready, the comforting presence of her brothers in arms on every side, each one ready to die for his country . . . or for Napoleon . . . . She fell asleep.

On Friday afternoon Peggy decided she needed some new clothes. She would go shopping and leave Nigel in charge of the shop. Nigel was rather annoyed. After all, he was on holiday and although there was not much for him to be doing down here, he rather fancied the idea of another trip to Exeter himself. Never mind, he didn't wish to cause an argument. He would look after the shop.

Peggy prepared to leave. While Nigel was at it, he might dust a few of the shelves. You had no idea how much time it took to keep the place clean. Mrs Chedzoy really ought to come in more often.

Nigel had no intention of dusting the shelves. All the tins of baked beans were sticky and he didn't fancy the idea of all that mess on his hands. Josephine and Jack went off to the garage. Josephine was delighted. She had to do her mother's dirty work often enough and she didn't see why it shouldn't be Nigel's turn.

Friday was a busy afternoon. Nigel was amazed by the number of people who came in and out of the shop. They all wanted to stop and talk which was very tiring. They seemed to want to know every detail of Nigel's life.

'I suppose you see more of your dad, that's to say Mrs Bennett's first husband,' one woman remarked. Nigel pretended not to hear. It took him all his time to remember where everything was kept.

It was not until just before five that a police car drew up outside the shop. Nigel saw two policemen climb out of the front of the car. They came straight into the shop and said that they wanted to question a young man who was said to be staying there.

Nigel was completely nonplussed. He had only been in Chadcombe for a few days. What on earth could they want with him? No, he was permanently employed in London and had been at work on all of the first three days they mentioned. They had only to check with his employers. Had he been in Exeter on Tuesday? Let him think. No, not Tuesday. He did go there briefly on Monday afternoon, but not on Tuesday. Yes, he could find his stepfather who would certainly speak for him. Would the two officers mind waiting a moment?

No, Jack couldn't for the life of him remember which day Nigel had gone to Exeter. He'd been busy with his soldiers himself and one day was very like another. Of course if Nigel said it was Monday, it must have been Monday. He would know. Jack had a pretty low opinion of police methods and he thought they must be wasting the tax-payer's money, coming round to bother a decent fellow like Nigel, just because he was new in the neighbourhood. He wondered what had led them to Chadcombe in the first place. He told Josephine to wait in the garage and returned to the shop with Nigel.

The police officers appeared to be satisfied when Jack assured them that Nigel had not been to Exeter on Tuesday. There had, they said, been rather a lot of indecent exposure cases in the last few months and since the matter was mentioned on the regional news the police had been inundated with calls from people making helpful suggestions. Someone had mentioned Nigel. Busybodies in country villages with nothing better to do. The two policemen were driving through Chadcombe so they thought they might put in a routine call. But then it was a waste of time really, since Nigel lived in London. He could hardly be the guilty party under the circumstances, now could he? The two policemen apologised for having bothered him and left almost immediately.

Peggy arrived home just as the police car drove away.

'Well, they could be out catching flashers – not hanging around here wasting everybody's time,' she said tartly. 'What did they come for anyway?'

'Something to do with a hit and run driver – but I explained that I don't have a car,' said Nigel.

On his way out of the back of the shop Jack met Josephine. He wondered what she was doing. He hadn't wanted her to be frightened by the police. She should have stayed where she was.

Josephine gave Jack a sideways look.

'Why did you say that Nigel went to Exeter on Monday, Daddy? You know he went on Tuesday.'

Chapter V

Somehow Jack was beginning to feel his age. It was about four years now since he had retired. Time went by so quickly. Josephine was fourteen and a half and he – well, that didn't bear thinking about. He'd be seventy next year. He couldn't deny that he was beginning to feel out of breath at times. But he was almost more annoyed by an increasing stiffness in the joints. He didn't really care to walk down to the pub without a stick any longer. What a damned nuisance old age was to be sure. Younger people didn't seem to have any conception of how inconvenient it was.

Jack was shortly due to drive over to Josephine's school for parents' day and to bring her home for the summer holidays. Peggy was trying to persuade him to take it slowly. He was planning to spend a night with the Browns – that nice couple he had made such friends with on the cruise and who lived not far from the school. Peggy felt he ought to make a complete break and take an extra day. It was a long drive and he would tire himself out if he came back straight away. The Browns were always urging him to stay. They would be only too delighted to have him a little longer.

It was nice of Peggy to be so considerate and Jack thought that she was probably right. After all he was not as young as he had been. He would get in touch with the Browns.

The Browns lived in a small village house just outside St Albans. Maurice Brown had spent most of his life as a solicitor in that town. It was a nice house but the neighbourhood was pretty built up. Not like the West Country.

Jack was quite shocked when he saw Maurice. They had exchanged Christmas greetings over the years and at intervals the Bennetts had received post cards from the Browns – from Cyprus, Luxor, the Seychelles or Sicily – but they had not met since the Greek cruise four years earlier.

Maurice Brown was several years older than Jack. His bent
and ageing appearance caught the Major off his guard. The
heavily veined, arthritic hand which clasped the knob of the
walking stick seemed to be saying, 'Look at me. This is the way
of all flesh. You don't have much longer yourself.'

It took Maurice Brown a painfully long time to shuffle
from the sitting room to the dining room for supper. Daphne
Brown walked beside him, her hand supporting him by the
elbow. With a twinge of disgust Jack noticed a thin line of
saliva trickling from the corner of Maurice's mouth. Jack may
well have been feeling his age lately, but he certainly looked
a good deal younger than poor, old Maurice. He would be
the first to admit that he might be getting a little stiff, but he
still had a straight back. Quite a military bearing. And of
course he had never had the misfortune to lose his hair.
Come to think of it he had a better head of hair than many a
younger man.

The Browns had a really nice dining room. Jack sat down
next to Maurice while Daphne went to the sideboard to serve
the soup.

'What delightful table mats,' Jack remarked, adjusting his
spectacles so as to admire more closely the pied flycatcher so
carefully reproduced in front of him.

'Oh, you've got the pied flycatcher!' exclaimed Daphne, and
immediately hid it beneath a plate of soup. 'Aren't they pretty?
Our daughter gave them to us.'

'Do let me see what you've got,' said Jack, craning his neck,
'before you cover it up.'

Daphne had a reed bunting and Maurice had a sedge
warbler. They really were most attractive. Daphne could
never make up her mind which one she liked best.

'Most attractive. Most attractive,' muttered poor Maurice
as, with a trembling hand, he lifted his spoon to his mouth.

Jack was tired after his long journey, but the sherry, the
claret, the excellent dinner, the charming dining room, the
reproduction Georgian table and the French windows, and the
change of scene all contributed to a feeling of well-being. The
change of scene was particularly welcome. He felt sorry for

Peggy, left behind to manage the shop. She might have enjoyed the evening.

Daphne had made a first-class cottage pie with twice-cooked meat.

'It's easily digestible for Maurice,' she said.

Jack looked nervously at Maurice who appeared not to have heard. He was pushing his cottage pie messily around his plate.

'Remember Sounion?' Maurice suddenly asked. 'It's beautiful, that little temple. But I still think I prefer some of the Sicilian sites. You really ought to go to Sicily. You'd love the place . . . .'

'I hope we manage to get away in October,' Daphne interrupted. 'Of course it all depends on Maurice's health.'

'Don't you worry about my health,' Maurice snarled. 'I'll be all right for a few years yet.'

Jack wondered how much younger than Maurice Daphne was. Very little, probably. But she was well preserved and still full of energy. He would put her at a spry seventy-five.

After supper Daphne helped Maurice upstairs. Jack, too, felt that he would like an early night. It had been a long drive. He thanked Daphne for the excellent meal and complimented her on her cooking. As he climbed the stairs to bed, he wondered how many years it would be before he too would need a helping hand.

The next morning Jack was downstairs at half past eight. He wore cavalry twill trousers, a blazer and his regimental tie. The toes of his shoes shone like two highly polished conkers. Daphne thought he looked very smart. Not quite as tall as Maurice, but a nice-looking man all the same. Daphne herself was dressed in a pale blue linen dress to match her eyes. She had been up for some time, clearing away the supper and laying the breakfast for two in the kitchen.

'Maurice has his breakfast upstairs. He has done since he had his stroke,' she explained.

'I was sorry to hear he had been unwell,' said Jack.

'He has to take such care nowadays,' Daphne went on. 'And then he's become so irritable. He never used to be like that before . . . . Would you like a boiled egg?'

'That would be lovely. But Maurice's health must be a worry for you.'

Yes, it was a worry for Daphne. She was always afraid he would over-do things. And of course he looked so much older physically. Jack must have noticed the change. Daphne had to admit that she had always been very lucky with her health. She had had a really bad bout of 'flu in the spring, but apart from that she couldn't remember spending a day in bed for years.

'And I shall be seventy-four next week,' she said proudly.

'Good gracious me!' exclaimed Jack. 'I imagined you were only in your late sixties. I was certain you were younger than me. I'm just coming seventy.'

Daphne glowed with pleasure.

'That's very kind of you,' she said, opening her blue eyes wide.

Jack helped himself to pepper and salt and began to butter his toast. What a nice time he was having and what a good idea it had been to invite himself for that extra day.

'I'm so glad you came,' said Daphne. 'We do have friends round here, but one can't go bothering them all the time and it can be lonely. Perhaps it's something to do with growing old. Don't you get lonely down in Devon?'

Jack couldn't understand why on earth he should be lonely. He had a wife, and Josephine in the holidays. He had his soldiers – and he could never be lonely with them – his books, and a few cronies in the pub. Lonely. No, he didn't think he was ever particularly lonely. He had certainly been lonely after his first wife died. But that was only to be expected. In any case he had married again quite soon. He thought perhaps Daphne was lonely because she was forced by her husband's ill-health to lead a quieter life than she had been used to.

'I think poor Maurice is lonely too,' she said. 'After all you do feel lonely when you're ill, don't you? I remember when I had 'flu. I felt so low I couldn't even read a book. I just lay there feeling sorry for myself. And then Maurice must be frightened too a lot of the time. Of course he would never admit it. But he must worry about what would happen if he had another stroke. Fear and loneliness are closely related. Oh well, I mustn't bore you with all this.' Daphne began to clear the table.

Jack was surprised by the frank way she spoke. What an intelligent and understanding person she was. How lucky for Maurice to have such a wife. He wondered how Peggy would behave with a sick husband. Well there was no point in worrying about that before he was ill. Sufficient unto the day . . . .

Daphne was piling plates in the sink. Jack offered to help her wash up the breakfast but Daphne assured him that her daily help would be there shortly, so he said he would take himself for a walk in the village. Have a look around. Come back and glance at the papers. Daphne told him that her daughter-in-law had invited them all to lunch. She lived in a nearby village.

The day was spent pleasantly. Jack liked the Browns' daughter-in-law who was welcoming and friendly. In the afternoon he admired Daphne's garden while Maurice rested. Daphne loved her garden and spent many hours tending it. Jack admired the beautiful white lilies which grew among deep purple lavender. He was not much of a gardener himself but he had to admire Daphne's handiwork.

It was a sunny day and after tea Maurice and Jack sat in the garden enjoying the sweet summer scents and talking of this and that.

Maurice was a sick man but he had not lost his interest in the world. He still remembered every detail of the places he had visited and the books he had read but he was deeply frustrated by his inability to do the things he used to do. It was a blasted nuisance moving so slowly. He liked to take a little walk every day. But he couldn't go far and he was painfully aware that he travelled at a snail's pace. Besides people tended to treat you like a baby or a simpleton. It was good of Jack to have come to see them. Poor Daphne was as fit as a fiddle – young as a spring chicken – she must be bored to death looking after a semi-invalid. But there it was. She never complained and we would all come to it in the end one way or another. Well, there was October to look forward to. The Browns were planning another trip to Sicily. A quiet hotel by the seaside, then they'd hire a car and a driver for a little sight-seeing. Daphne would see to it that they took things gently.

The following morning Jack, dressed in his best suit, said good-bye to the Browns and thanked them from the bottom of his heart. He had really enjoyed the visit and he sincerely hoped that the Browns would see their way to visiting Devon in the near future.

42

He drove off to Josephine's school where a fork lunch and prize-giving awaited him. He was proud of Josephine who had won a history prize, a mathematics prize, a Latin prize and her form prize. The school was so far away that Peggy and Jack rarely visited it. Josephine usually went back and forth by train. But Jack felt that she worked so well and gained so many prizes that it was time for at least one of her parents to be there to applaud as she stepped up to the platform.

The prizes were to be presented by the wife of the Conservative member of Parliament for the constituency.

Josephine dreaded the arrival of her father. She had written almost begging him not to come. He must be the oldest father in the school and she already had enough problems as a result of being cleverer, fatter and poorer than most of the other girls. She had told her father that nobody's parents came to prize-giving, which would be rather embarrassing when he saw them all milling into the school. In other years she had stood alone on the edge of the gathering, observing girls and their parents, feeling isolated in the crowd but glad that her mother and father had not come and, to a certain extent, superior in the knowledge of her academic successes.

This year was different. Jack had insisted on coming and Josephine knew that it was because he loved her and was proud of her. She loved him too, but he belonged at home in Devon. She woke on the last morning of term with a sick feeling in the pit of her stomach. Only a few more hours and her father would be there to embarrass her.

There were eight beds in the dormitory. Josephine lay quite still and listened to two other girls gossiping.

'Only two more days till I can see Marcus,' said one.

'My parents have said that we can have a barbecue and disco beside the swimming pool before we go to Spain,' said the other.

'Gosh you lucky thing!'

'The only trouble is that I've got to share it with this cousin and she's such a frightful tart. I fancied this boy and she . . . .' They went on and on and on. Josephine knew nothing of their world and they, she supposed, knew nothing of hers.

On the other side of the room two more girls were talking in loud voices about ponies. Spindle jumped beautifully and Misty who was half-Arab had a lovely head.

Josephine sat up and stretched. She wished Misty and Spindle would both die.

'Hey Josephine,' called one of the girls, 'cheer up, we're going home today. No more stinking maths and biology. Oh, sorry, you'll probably miss them. Going anywhere exciting this holidays?'

'I expect so,' Josephine lied.

'Are your parents coming to prize-giving?' asked a blonde girl.

Josephine was standing by her bed, tying a camel-coloured acrylic dressing-gown around her.

'My father is.'

'So's my mother. My sister's boyfriend's got a sports car.'

Josephine wondered how the two statements were connected. She picked up her sponge bag and wandered off in the direction of the bathroom. When she came back the blonde girl was busy painting her eyes.

'You really ought to wear eye-liner you know,' the blonde advised Josephine.

'I don't think my parents would let me,' said Josephine.

'You don't have to tell them, stupid.'

'Anyway I don't see the point at school.'

'You want to look your best at all times, don't you? And anyway, not wishing to be beastly, if you've got quite a fat face – I mean not that you're fat or anything – but if you have got a biggish sort of face and well not specially big eyes, eye-liner would really suit you. It'd make your eyes look much bigger.'

'Thanks for the few kind words,' said Josephine.

'You can borrow mine,' said the blonde with a sudden impulse of generosity.

'No thanks,' said Josephine sourly. She put on her spectacles and picked up *Under the Greenwood Tree* from the locker beside her bed. She hated them all. They were so silly. She would have liked a friend. But not one of them. She left the dormitory.

'Poor old Josephine,' said one of the pony owners. 'Why don't her parents give her some decent clothes?'

'They're too poor,' explained her friend. 'And do you know, if she ever asks for anything new her father strips her naked and whips her. I absolutely promise it's true. Swear on the Holy Bible. Sally told me.'

'Gosh, poor her, how awful! Still if they can afford to send her to this school then they can jolly well afford to give her some nice things.'

'D'you think she's ever been kissed?' asked someone.

'Ugh! Who'd want to kiss her,' said the blonde who had never been kissed either.

The morning passed slowly for Josephine. She just wished the day would end. She sat in her classroom reading a book and glancing from time to time at her watch. Parents were due to start arriving at eleven when they were to be shown around the school. There was an excellent display in the art room. At twelve o'clock there would be lunch and prize-giving was to begin at a quarter to two. In every corner of the school groups of excited girls giggled and gossiped and looked at their reflections in window panes or in the glass covering the reproductions of old masters which adorned every corridor and classroom.

Girls brought tiny brushes out of pockets and purses and endlessly brushed their hair, sucking in their cheeks and raising their eye-brows as they did so.

At last the cars began to arrive. As one girl disappeared to greet her parents others craned their necks to see out of windows.

'Gosh, have you seen Jacky's mother? She's hideous! She looks like a witch . . . .'

'Who's that old man?'

'Must be someone's grandfather.'

'Shut up, you fool. It's Josephine Bennett's father.'

There was a sound of stifled sniggering.

Jack was so proud of Josephine. He wanted to meet all her teachers and all her friends. At lunch she introduced him to her Latin teacher, Miss Hadley, who was a bit of an old bag but quite nice really.

Miss Hadley looked quite the part in her burgundy trouser suit with her hair scraped into a neat bun and her spectacles perched on her pointed nose. But Jack thought her intelligent

45

and charming. Josephine was one of her best pupils. The most promising child she had taught for a long time. She would do well and should certainly go on to university. Miss Hadley herself had been at Cambridge. She couldn't recommend too highly the advantages of a university education, and of course for a child like Josephine, university was an essential.

Josephine's heart swelled with pleasure as she listened to all the praise. Parents' day wasn't so bad after all. Later when she collected her prizes she had another moment of exhilarating joy. It was almost as though all the loneliness and misery of school were worth it for the brief moment, once a year, when she stood up in front of everyone and was applauded. Jack clapped loudest.

Then came the long drive home. Josephine began to wonder how she was going to spend the holidays. Most of the other girls at school seemed to be going to Spain or Greece – or even Cornwall. One was going to Kenya. The ones who were staying at home seemed to be engrossed in ponies and three-day events.

'Why don't you ask a friend to stay in the holidays to keep you company?' Jack suggested.

Josephine didn't think that that was a very good idea so she made a number of excuses, none of which seemed very convincing to Jack. She could hardly say that there was nobody whom she dared to ask, or knew well enough to ask. Nor could she very well say that she hated everyone at school. She didn't think she could say that the girls at school would think it very odd living in a shop. Besides there was nothing to do at home. There was no tennis court, no swimming pool. Not that Josephine had any desire to play tennis. She hated games. She didn't particularly want to go swimming either, not because she disliked swimming – in fact she quite enjoyed it – but because she felt fat and ugly in a bathing-suit. For an instant she imagined that she would gladly relinquish all her prizes to be thin and ordinary just like everyone else. But at the same time she knew she would loathe the indignity of not being the cleverest.

'Well,' said Jack kindly, 'what are we going to do to keep you occupied?' He wished she would agree to invite one of her little friends and wondered why she had been so reluctant to introduce them to him at school. He, of course, would take her out and about – to the seaside and perhaps to the theatre. They were doing *Henry V* at the Northcote. Jack enjoyed his outings with Josephine.

Josephine's mind turned to her father's model soldiers. It was a long time since they had laid out a battle together.

'We can always play with the soldiers,' she said.

They drove on in silence, both absorbed in private thought.

Chapter VI

When Peggy first moved to Chadcombe she had no friends in the neighbourhood. There was only her mother who lived in a ground-floor flat in a terraced house near the centre of Exeter. She had never cared much for her mother but had used her off and on over the years as a baby-sitter, first for Nigel and later for Josephine. Whenever she wanted to go away she had either sent her children to stay with Mrs Baker or Mrs Baker had come to stay with her.

Now that Peggy lived so close to her mother she saw her more often. She would pop in for a cup of tea after shopping in Exeter and usually come away irritated. Mrs Baker was over eighty and beginning to show her age, but Peggy had little patience with what she regarded as self-pity and therefore little sympathy for her mother. Did her mother really expect to run around like a forty-year-old at her age?

Thirty years earlier, after her husband's premature death, Mrs Baker had retired to Exeter from the Midlands. She had heard that the climate was milder in the West Country and she also felt that she needed to make a completely new start. Her husband had left her moderately well off, but she used to earn a little pin-money by working part-time in a wool shop and for many years she had helped with meals on wheels. For the last few years she had herself been a recipient of meals on wheels. She didn't particularly fancy the meals but such a nice young woman came round with Wednesday's dinner that she really looked forward to Wednesdays.

Apart from Wednesdays, there was very little that Mrs Baker did look forward to. Her daughter, Peggy, aggravated her by her selfishness and tired her with complaints. Josephine, whom she saw once or twice each holidays, was an

48

unattractive child – rather sour and stand-offish, Mrs Baker thought. It was difficult to be fond of her.

According to Peggy, Josephine was very clever, but then you could never believe a word Peggy said. She used to say Jack was clever but now she said that Jack had become stupid all of a sudden – quite in his dotage – and very selfish. No, Mrs Baker couldn't honestly say that she looked forward to seeing either Peggy or Josephine except in so far as they interrupted the monotony of day succeeding day.

More than anything else, Mrs Baker looked forward to dying. She looked forward to dying even more than she looked forward to Wednesdays. Let it come quickly.

Beyond the grave Mrs Baker imagined oblivion or sometimes, when she was in a sentimental mood, she imagined being reunited with her husband or with her sister, Mildred, who had died before the war.

Mrs Baker was sitting as usual by the electric fire in her sitting room. It was chilly for the time of year and she badly felt the cold so she had a rug over her knees. She was trying to read. Her sight had been deteriorating rapidly lately, but a kind neighbour had brought her some books with especially large print. Even they were not always easy to read. She had had the glass removed from the front of the clock on the table beside her. She felt the hands. Five o'clock. And she was sure it was Thursday – that nice young woman had been around with the dinner yesterday. Or was it yesterday? It seemed much longer ago. Well if she was right and it was Thursday, Peggy would probably be looking in presently, it being early closing day in Chadcombe.

When Peggy arrived she was weighed down with parcels. She had been buying her summer wardrobe. She had found a gorgeous pair of white trousers in Dingles – quite reasonable too. Then she'd popped across to C & A to look for T-shirts. There were some lovely new shades this year. She had bought a cyclamen and a midnight blue.

'Aren't you rather old for that sort of thing, dear?' Mrs Baker asked. 'I mean you wouldn't want to look like mutton dressed as lamb.'

Peggy was furious. Mutton and lamb didn't come into it.

'I can afford to wear trousers with my figure,' she snapped. 'It would be quite another matter for Josephine. Now I have to be careful what I buy for her.'

'I'll put the kettle on.' Mrs Baker rose carefully from her chair, felt around for her stick and moved slowly across the room to the door.

'I won't offer to make the tea myself,' said Peggy. 'It's impossible to find anything here. You never seem to keep your cups in the same place from one week to another.'

Mrs Baker always kept her cups in the same place. If she didn't she would have difficulty finding them herself – what with her failing eyesight. She prepared a tea-tray with pretty rosy china and opened a packet of fig-rolls.

'Be so good as to carry the tray through, dear,' she asked her daughter.

Peggy was gasping for a cup of tea. The crowded town and stuffy shops had exhausted her. She'd had a busy afternoon. She lit a cigarette and sunk into a wide armchair covered in faded cretonne. She remembered that chair in her childhood home in the Midlands. It was comfortable all right, but it was enough to remind anyone of Solihull. Peggy had insisted on buying a nice, modern three-piece suite when she and Jack moved to Chadcombe. Jack had been against the idea. He couldn't see anything wrong with the settee they'd had all along. Peggy could. It was a clumsy old thing, just like that armchair.

'When does Josephine come home?' Mrs Baker wanted to know.

Peggy explained that Jack had driven to fetch her from school. He was going to parents' day and would be away for a couple of nights. Peggy thought that Jack could have stayed away longer. It would have done him good and besides it would have given her a break. She may well have married him for better or worse, but she certainly didn't marry him for lunch every day.

'Well I don't suppose he's much trouble to cook for, is he, dear? I think you should consider yourself lucky to have a nice considerate husband who's forever running errands for you. And such a gentleman – Jack. At your age I was widowed.'

'I'm glad you think Jack's considerate. In my opinion he's just like all men. He agrees with you in front of your face and then, the minute your back's turned, he does the opposite. Considerate. Not at all.'

When did Jack last take her out to a meal or tell her she looked nice? Peggy wanted to know. Peggy had no idea what Jack's first wife looked like, but she would have been nearly seventy if she were alive now. Jack didn't seem to realise how lucky he was to have a young and active wife.

Mrs Baker looked sharply at her daughter and wondered just how lucky Jack was.

'What are you getting up to while he's away?' she asked.

'Getting up to? I like that! There's nothing to get up to in a village like Chadcombe. I can't think what made us choose to come and live down here.'

In Mrs Baker's opinion life was what you made it.

'Well, I could do with a holiday,' said Peggy. 'June and I are thinking of going to the Costa Brava for a week. It all depends on whether or not I can find someone to look after the post office.'

June was Peggy's best friend. She owned a hairdresser's shop, which was where Peggy had met her. June was divorced and lived alone. Peggy found her friend's situation enviable although June said that Peggy should be grateful for the security which marriage brought. June could be ever so lonely at times – when she was between men.

Mrs Baker sniffed.

'What about Jack? Doesn't he want a holiday?'

'Jack doesn't care for sun-bathing and anyway I wouldn't want to leave the shop entirely alone in the hands of a stranger.'

'I sometimes wonder what brought you two together,' said Mrs Baker.

How dare she talk like that, Peggy demanded. Jack had been a godsend after Nigel's father had left. He'd really treated her like a lady. Taken her out of herself. Mrs Baker had no need to be rude about Jack. Jack was a very intelligent man and a gentleman. It wasn't his fault he was old. Of course old people didn't want to gad around the way younger people did. And it was a well known fact that old people became selfish. It was

51

part of their condition. Peggy glowered at her mother. She would probably be selfish herself by the time she was Jack's age. But one thing about Peggy was that she had never looked her age. Nor felt it for that matter. She didn't feel a day over thirty now.

Mrs Baker felt tired. She wished Peggy would go. It was always the same. Her daughter wore her out.

'Well,' said Peggy, looking at her watch, 'I must be going, or I'll miss the bus. Is there anything you want before I go?'

'No thank you dear, you run along and catch your bus.'

'I'll see you next week then,' said Peggy. 'If there's anything you want you can always ring.'

'Don't you worry about me. My neighbour will be in in the morning. She's ever so good to me.'

When Peggy had gone Mrs Baker leaned back in her chair and closed her eyes. Before long she was asleep. She woke about an hour later and was annoyed to notice her tea-cup was still on the table by her side. She should have asked Peggy to take the tea things back to the kitchen. It would take her such a long time to do it herself. Never mind. She had nothing else to do.

By the time Peggy reached home it was nearly half past seven. She really should have caught an earlier bus, but then she wouldn't have had time to see her mother. Her mother was tiresome and old but Peggy thought it would be unkind not to look in from time to time just to cheer the old girl up.

It was a pleasure to have the house to herself for once. She relished Josephine's and Jack's absence. She felt young and free. But she must hurry or she would be late. She wondered if her new white trousers would do but decided instead on a skin-tight lilac dress with white accessories. She was only just ready when she heard a car draw up outside and then, a few moments later, the front-door bell.

'Come on in then, Bruce,' said Peggy, as she opened the door.

He came into the sitting-room and she offered him a gin and tonic.

'Cheers!' Bruce raised his glass.

52

'Cheers!'

'I've ordered a table at a place I know out in the country. Take us about twenty-five minutes to get there, but it's nice. They do a nice *sole Véronique* – do you like fish?'

Peggy thought that the only trouble with fish was the bones.

'They do good steaks, too. French style.'

This, thought Peggy, is the life. She looked at Bruce. He was a really nice looking bloke. Just the sort she had always fancied. For a fleeting moment he reminded her of her first husband, but she put the thought quickly out of her mind.

As they left the house Bruce caught sight of his reflection in a mirror which hung just inside the front-door. He patted his thick grey hair and stuck out his chin. He liked his red turtle-necked jersey.

Peggy had never been out with Bruce before although she had known him for some time. She had met him on and off with June. His wife worked in June's shop and was a friend of hers. Until a few years ago Bruce had worked for a firm which made spare parts for tractors. When the firm went out of business there weren't many jobs around, so Bruce decided to become his own boss – go it alone – and before long he had set himself up as a driving instructor. It had been a bit of a hassle at the time but lately things had begun to look up and Bruce was pretty busy. He lived in Exeter with his wife and teen-aged daughter.

It was a pity about the car, Peggy thought as they bowled through the countryside. She would have preferred something silver and a little more stream-lined. Even a two-seater. You felt a bit of a charlie with all those 'L' plates.

Over dinner Bruce confided in Peggy. It was really good of her to agree to come out with him. He had been thinking of her all week and looking forward to their evening together. He hadn't been getting on at all well with his wife lately. He suspected her of having a boy-friend. Not that it would be the first time. He could understand her, mind you. He was a busy man, and it hadn't been easy building up the business over the last few years. Of course he had neglected his wife. He would be the first person to take the blame. But he didn't want to talk about himself. He wanted to know all about Peggy. What was an attractive woman like Peggy doing in a hidden away place like Chadcombe?

One look at the menu was enough for Peggy to decide that she would have to forget about dieting for the evening. There were at least ten different starters to choose from before you even began to think about *sole Véronique* or whatever.

Peggy finally settled for the avocado with prawns *à la Santa Lucia*. When she thought about the evening later she couldn't remember what Bruce had chosen.

'I really don't know what to have next.' Peggy gazed in confusion at the menu, which was at least as big as the *Sunday Express*, if not so easy to read.

'How about the little baby small spring *poussins* – baby chickens, Madam – tossed in butter, *flambé*-ed in Pernod, stewed in milk with a dash of cinnamon, served with a cream and brandy sauce and a garnish of mushrooms, shrimps and asparagus tips on a bed of fresh green lettuce with an accompaniment of continental vegetables – baby carrots, specially selected garden peas, boiled and creamed potatoes and *zucchini*, Madam – Italian baby marrows.'

That sounded lovely.

Peggy had no room for a dessert after all that which was a shame really. The chocolate *gâteau* looked smashing.

Bruce promised to bring her back again another day.

After dinner the two sat smoking and sipping liqueurs. After Eights were served with the liqueurs. They were in no hurry to go back to Chadcombe. They had the whole night before them. Bruce had fabricated some lie to account for his absence to his wife.

'That was a really gorgeous dinner,' said Peggy. 'Jack and I hardly ever go out. He always says it's extravagant to go to restaurants.'

'Nothing's too extravagant for a pretty woman like you,' said Bruce. 'Anyway, if I have learned anything from life, I've learned one thing and what I've learned is that there's no use in money if you don't spend it – well you can't take it with you when you go, now can you? Now look at it this way, we've only got one life, haven't we? Well, that's the way I see it. So it must be our duty to enjoy this life as much as we can, make the best of it, well, we won't be getting another chance, will we?' He pushed his leg against Peggy's under the table. Peggy giggled and applied a faint pressure in return.

Bruce decided that the time had come to call for the bill. He snapped his fingers casually in the direction of the waiter, but when the bill came and he glanced at the total he didn't feel nearly so casual. He found himself obliged to affect an air of nonchalance as he signed an enormous cheque. He hoped to God it was going to be worth it. He could hardly afford many more meals like this one.

They sped home carelessly through the lanes. They had had two bottles of wine and several liqueurs not to mention the cocktails to start with. Peggy was decidedly a little drunk. She was laughing a lot and saying 'You are a one' or 'As the bishop said to the actress' in answer to anything Bruce said.

'You make me feel twenty again,' she said as the car swerved round a sharp bend on two wheels.

'It's quite safe at night . . . .'

'As the bishop said to the actress,' said Peggy.

'If anything's coming you can see the headlights.'

Bruce put his foot down and accelerated into the straight.

Peggy stretched her legs out in front of her. She was glad she had such long and seductive legs and such slim ankles. Bruce put a hand on her knee.

By the time they reached Chadcombe it was time for a night-cap. Peggy found a bottle of Cointreau left over from Christmas, lurking in the back of a cupboard. She slopped some out for each of them.

'Cheers,' she said.

'Cheers,' he said and they clinked glasses. But instead of drinking, Bruce put his glass down and drew Peggy to him in a greedy embrace causing her to spill her drink everywhere.

'Oh bother the drink,' said Peggy as he finally released her. 'Let's go upstairs.'

The next morning Peggy had a dreadful headache. She felt like death when she was woken by the sound of snoring. One thing to be said for Jack was that he never snored. Oh well. Never mind. You couldn't have everything in life, and she had enjoyed herself last night. She looked at the clock and was surprised to see that it was already half past seven.

Bruce turned over in bed beside her. She'd better wake him. She wanted him gone before Mrs Chedzoy turned up with her nose in everybody else's business.

Bruce was horrified by the lateness of the hour. He had to be at work by half-past eight. He must fly.

Bleary-eyed, Peggy staggered down to the kitchen to put on a kettle. Her head was pounding. It was all those liqueurs. She wasn't used to drinking liqueurs. She lit a cigarette. That should make her feel better.

By the time Bruce came down she had managed to lay the table and make some tea and toast. He hardly had time to swallow the tea.

'So when does hubby get back?' he asked with a wink as he stood up to leave.

'Tonight,' said Peggy, 'and Josephine too.'

'We'll manage,' said Bruce, 'don't worry.'

'I did my best to persuade him to stay away longer,' she said.

'I'll give you a ring.' He kissed her, squeezed her hand and winked again. 'Nothing like a bit of fun,' he said and was gone.

When Peggy had removed all the evidence of breakfast for two she went back upstairs. She had time for a little lie in before she need open the shop.

Bruce let himself out of the front door and was about to get into his car when a bright West Country voice wished him good morning.

'It looks like a nice day,' said Mrs Yeo. 'Are you staying with the Bennetts then?'

'No, not at all. Oh no,' said Bruce. 'I was just dropping a packet in for the Major.'

'The Major's away.'

'Oh yes, well he'll find it when he gets back.'

'I could have sworn I saw your car there last night,' said Mrs Yeo. 'Funny, I must be mistaken, and I'm not usually mistaken

56

about things like that.'

'Well you're mistaken this time,' snapped Bruce as he slammed the car door.

He was prevented from making a quick get-away by a tractor which was coming slowly towards him and blocking the entire road. Mrs Yeo stood watching him while he waited.

Peggy swallowed two aspirins and examined her face in the bathroom mirror before dragging herself back to bed. She was shocked by the sight of her drawn, grey skin and the bags under her eyes. For a moment she looked her age. She thought of the future and was afraid. She had told Bruce that she was forty-six and it hadn't crossed her mind that he wouldn't believe her. He was fifty-four. Or had he lied too?

She crawled into bed. The pillow-case smelled of Bruce's after-shave. She must remember to change it before Jack came back. Not that he would notice. Jack never noticed anything any more. Now Bruce – Bruce noticed everything. He noticed her dress, her hair, her perfume – Bruce was the sort of man that made a woman feel good. Not that she felt particularly good this morning. She wished Bruce could have stayed longer. It was horrid him having to hurry away like that. She felt tired, abandoned and miserable. Why wasn't Jack there to bring her a nice, strong cup of coffee?

Poor old Jack. What on earth would he have thought if he could have seen her last night? He would have been amazed. She was quite amazed herself. After all, Chadcombe was not exactly full of attractive and available men. She should know. She had been looking for one for some time now. She was lucky to have met Bruce at last. No, it wasn't at all easy to find a lover if you lived in the country with a husband who was always at home. She wondered when Bruce would telephone. She wondered if he was rich. He'd certainly spent enough on her dinner. It was a nice restaurant too. What you might call high-class. Definitely high-class. She heard the church clock strike a quarter to nine. The last thing you wanted to hear when you had a headache was the church clock. Or any other clock for that matter. She stretched out a hand to the bedside table for a cigarette. Then she fumbled for some matches. Drat! She was sure she had some. She found them and lit her cigarette. As she

57

inhaled deeply her stomach gave a lurch. She thought she was
going to be sick.

Oh, my God, she thought, why isn't there anyone here to
look after me? She wondered what time Jack would be back.

Chapter VII

As far as Nigel could see there was only one way of putting an end to his association with Suzanne. He would have to change his job.

Just the other week-end, at her parents' house – on a Sunday – her mother had started making the usual pointed remarks. But this time she had gone too far. Nigel didn't know where to look.

'If your mother's anything like myself, Nigel,' said Mrs Evans, 'then she'll be thinking it's about time she had some grandchildren.'

Nigel didn't think his mother was particularly interested in grandchildren. Nor did he think she was anything like Mrs Evans. It occurred to him that in fact he hadn't spoken to her, or even seen her, for a long time. Well, they'd exchanged cards at Christmas. He had even sent her a tea towel with a recipe for *Boeuf Stroganoff* on it. But he hadn't been down to Chadcombe for several years. It must be nearly four now. Not since that embarrassing occasion when the police called so uncomfortably at the shop. He didn't care to dwell on that, and as a result the very thought of Chadcombe made him feel uneasy. He had no urge to return there in a hurry. Peggy had been to London once or twice. She sometimes came up on a day return with a woman friend of hers – a hairdresser. They had all three lunched together a couple of times in a coffee shop near the department store.

'I'm quite surprised, I really am,' Mrs Evans went on, 'that you haven't thought to invite Suzanne home. I should hardly think you could count the number of times she's brought you here.' Mrs Evans's knitting needles clicked aggressively. Her orange wool was almost fluorescent. Nigel wished she would be quiet. The film on television was quite interesting – or would be if only he were allowed to pay attention to it.

59

'Oh, Mum', said Suzanne, 'be quiet, can't you. We're trying to watch the telly.'

'I'm only speaking on your behalf, dear. I expect you would like to meet Nigel's parents. Wouldn't you?' Mrs Evans glared at her daughter. It was a pity that Suzanne had inherited her father's huge beaky nose. It dominated her whole face. You hardly noticed her eyes. And what a shame about her complexion. She should be past the age of having all those spots. The trouble was that she never stopped eating chocolates. Mrs Evans had told her about it often enough, but then the young these days always knew best.

'I should think your people would be pleased to meet Suzanne too,' said Mrs Evans. 'After all you've been going out together now for what is it – four years? Five?' Mrs Evans knew exactly how long they had been going out together. 'And none of us is getting any younger,' she added lamely.

Nigel pretended not to hear. Suzanne unwrapped a Crunchie bar and began to munch it noisily.

'You'll do yourself no good with all those chocolates you eat,' said her mother.

'Oh, Mum,' said Suzanne, 'can't you leave me alone. I'm not a kid any more, you know.'

Never mind a kid. Suzanne was twenty-seven. If they left it much longer she'd be past child-bearing age. Mrs Evans couldn't see the sense in it. Nigel was a nice boy really. Look at the bunch of red tulips he'd brought her that morning. And he was ever so polite. Always said thank you nicely for his Sunday dinner. But what on earth was he waiting for? Mrs Evans often wondered what Nigel and Suzanne got up to together – if anything. Sometimes she thought there must be something wrong with the man. Perhaps he was under-sexed. Well you never knew, did you? And Suzanne wasn't giving anything away. She was a cagey one.

The television film came to an end and Suzanne suggested making a pot of tea. As she walked out of the room it occurred to Nigel that she had put on weight. Her jeans were too tight and you could see the line of her pants cutting across her backside. He couldn't imagine what Peggy would think of her if they ever did meet. His mother was always so smartly dressed. That was one thing you could say for Peggy.

Suzanne's father came into the room, rubbing his hands together.

'Lovely afternoon,' he said. 'A shame to be shut up in here when it's so nice out. I've tidied up the front garden. The scillas are all in bud. Be out in a day or two. You should see the forsythia at number twenty-eight. Beautiful. Mine never does as well as theirs. Good film?'

'Never mind forsythia,' said Mrs Evans. 'Suzanne's gone to make a nice cup of tea. Sit down, dear.'

Mr Evans rubbed his hands together again and sank into his favourite armchair. He had worked for the electricity board for nearly as many years as he could remember – in the accounts department. He was stuck indoors all week and really looked forward to spending his week-ends in the garden. The only trouble was that you could never rely on the weather.

'Nigel's thinking of taking Suzanne to see his parents in Devon,' Mrs Evans announced. She was amazed by her own daring, but someone had to say something – things had been going on for long enough. Not to say too long. It was ridiculous.

'That's nice,' said Mr Evans. He was glancing at a motoring magazine and only half-listening.

Nigel was appalled and could think of nothing to say. Luckily the door opened and Suzanne came clattering in with the tea.

But now she had started, Mrs Evans was not prepared to give in lightly. She told her daughter that Nigel was planning on inviting her to Devon in the summer, to meet his parents.

Suzanne's face lit up with surprise and pleasure.

'It depends on my mother,' said Nigel, finally defeated. 'I'll have to find out when it suits her.' He felt a sinking feeling in the pit of his stomach. He did not want to go back to Chadcombe and neither did he wish to introduce Suzanne to his mother and stepfather. Things were getting out of control. He supposed he would be able to make some excuse. Pretend Jack was ill. But he could hardly go on making excuses for ever. And there was the awkward matter of Suzanne's feelings. He quite liked Suzanne and didn't particularly wish to offend her. She had looked so happy when her mother had announced that Nigel was going to take her home that he hadn't dared to deny it.

As soon as he had finished his cup of tea, Nigel decided to make his get-away. Suzanne was sorry to see him leave so early and said she would go with him to the tube.

She slipped her hand through Nigel's arm as they walked towards the underground station. She felt so happy. She closed her mind to the fact that the invitation must have been manoeuvred by her mother. At least he really was going to take her home. That must mean something. He must care underneath.

Suzanne's friendship with Nigel had been making her more and more miserable for over a year now. Not only her mother, but almost everybody she knew seemed to be for ever dropping hints. Her father was all right. He minded his own business. But her aunties and her cousins – even the neighbours and the other girls at work, they were all nearly as bad as her mother. You'd think that none of them had anything else to interest them.

If Suzanne had been brave enough she would have finished with Nigel months ago. Years ago, probably. She tried to tell herself that she was in love with him. She was sure that if she lost him she would never find anyone else. She could see he was no Robert Redford. But he was kind and that was what counted. Look at the lovely bunch of tulips he had brought her mum that morning. Anyway she wasn't exactly pretty herself – and she was getting on for thirty now. She sometimes wondered where her youth had gone to. It had certainly been uneventful. Then her spots were a dreadful problem. She spent pounds on creams and lotions, but she knew that her mother was right really. It was the chocolates that did it. She wanted marriage and sex – not necessarily in that order – she wanted babies and she wanted to get away from her mother. Then she would easily be able to give up the confounded chocolates. But you had to have some comfort in life.

'Want a Rolo?' she asked Nigel as she delved into her coat pocket. They had reached the tube station without exchanging a word.

'No thanks, I'll be on my way. Thank you for the dinner.'

'Goodbye, love. Look after yourself. See you at work.' Suzanne turned to walk home. Tears pricked her eyes. He didn't even kiss her goodbye. It was hopeless. He hadn't mentioned

Devon again. He probably regretted ever having brought it up in the first place. And she would so love to go to Devon. All that cream and cider and the seaside. It sounded nice. Nicer than Cricklewood.

She walked slowly up the road. Tears had begun to stream down her cheeks. She put another Rolo in her mouth. And another. And another. She felt a bit better. A young woman walking towards her stared rudely at her falling tears. She scowled back disconsolately at the stranger who doubtless had a husband – a handsome lover – a baby – holidays in Spain. Her tears fell faster as she trudged towards home. She wished she had someone to confide in but she could not bear to reveal the truth to anyone, not even to Mandy, her friend at work.

She looked at her watch. It was too early to go home, so as it was a nice evening she decided to go for a walk. Anything rather than return to her mother.

An hour or so later Suzanne went into a pub and ordered a vodka and lime. She had walked a long way and felt calmer but no happier. Neither had she reached any decision. She would have a stiff drink before going home. Sitting alone in the corner of the pub with her vodka and a new packet or Rolos she began to cry again. She saw herself at forty – fifty – sixty, single, childless, unloved, plain and uninteresting. There was no way out. She didn't even have a very exciting job and there was not really any hope of a better one. Why was life so darned unfair? The other people in the pub were sitting or standing in groups, laughing and shouting. The barmaid with her yellow hair and huge bosom was laughing loudest of all and calling everyone 'luvey' and 'darling'. Suzanne hated them all.

When Nigel left Suzanne he took the tube to Picadilly Circus and then went to a dirty film. He was feeling thoroughly upset. Why did the whole world presume he should marry Suzanne? He had no intention of taking her to Chadcombe. The best thing would be just not to mention it again. She would never dare bring the subject up. The film helped him to forget his problems for the time being and when it was over he decided to go for a drink. It was early and he didn't feel like going straight back to his bed-sitter. The pub he chose was crowded and the atmosphere was cheerful. He thought he recognised a television personality. A lively place, Soho. He ordered a pint of beer and a couple of packets of salt and vinegar crisps.

Later on, after a third pint, he felt altogether more cheerful. There was nothing really to worry about. Least said, soonest mended as far as Suzanne was concerned. As for her mother, he wasn't afraid of her. Oh no. She needn't think she could bother him. He could stand up to her. He'd just tell her to mind her own business one of these days. Quite politely. But he'd tell her. There was no reason why he and Suzanne shouldn't go on as they were. After all they'd been perfectly happy for the last five years. Suzanne was quite nice. Not very pretty. Friendly and undemanding on the whole. A bit annoying at times – like when she nestled up beside him in the cinema – but still she could have been a lot worse. She had a nice home and he always appreciated the Sunday dinners he had there. He enjoyed a good meal from time to time. Mr Evans was a nice man too. Very welcoming, always made you feel at home, almost like one of the family. One of the family? Well, that was one thing he certainly didn't want to be. He smiled to himself. No, but seriously, he didn't really have much to worry about.

On the way back to Shepherd's Bush in the underground Nigel noticed two pretty young schoolgirls giggling and laughing together. Of course they didn't notice him. He had long ago learned that women never noticed him – well, not unless . . . . He groaned inwardly. No. He had promised himself to stop doing that. He knew what society thought of so-called 'flashers' and one day he might be caught. It had been a close thing down in Exeter. There would probably only be a fine – that wouldn't matter, but he didn't want that kind of notoriety. Not in the least. Besides he sometimes thought society was right. He felt ashamed of himself then and tried to resist temptation for long periods of time. Sometimes he succeeded for over a year. At other times he felt defiant. What harm could it possibly do, he wanted to know. Probably gave the girls a thrill. There was nothing to be frightened of. It wasn't as if he was going to rape anyone. Just a simple, innocent bit of fun to add spice to an otherwise uneventful life.

64

He glanced across the train at the giggling girls and felt the old, familiar surge of excitement. He hadn't done anything wrong for months now and, after all, it was Sunday night. Why not? For a moment his conscience pricked him and then he reached a compromise. Fate would decide. If the girls got out at Shepherd's Bush then he would follow them. If not, then he would regard it as a sign to leave them alone and behave himself.

The train rattled into Holland Park station. The two girls stood up. Damn it! Just my luck, thought Nigel.

The train stopped and the doors opened. The girls were about to get out when one pulled the other by the sleeve and squeaked. 'Come on, silly, we're not there yet. This is only Holland Park.'

At Shepherd's Bush Nigel followed them out of the train and out of the station. They were laughing and chatting and appeared not to notice him behind them. He followed them for some time, down Goldhawk Road and into the smaller streets leading off it. They reached a quiet, empty road and Nigel quickened his pace. He crossed the road, walked on and overtook the girls before crossing back to their side of the street and turning to walk towards them. Luckily there was a road off to his right down which he could make a quick getaway, back towards Goldhawk Road and the world. His excitement mounted as he approached the two girls. His hands were deep in his mackintosh pockets. He came to within a yard of them, just underneath a street light, and in the twinkling of an eye it was all over.

As Nigel ran back towards Goldhawk Road he heard screams behind him. He thought for one dreadful moment that he also heard pounding footsteps chasing him. It seemed like an age but in fact it was only a few minutes before he was back in civilisation. It was Sunday evening and the streets were hardly crowded but there was traffic and movement and in no time he was on a bus travelling calmly back towards Shepherd's Bush Green.

The next morning Nigel awoke feeling let down. It was always the same. A moment of squalid self-awareness in which he questioned his actions and then a warm flood of pleasure as he remembered the thrill, the triumph of himself over the dreary world in which he lived. Then the pleasure drained away and depression set in as he drank his mug of Nescafé. He had a

65

headache and felt slightly sick. Perhaps the last two pints before bed had been too much. He thought of the day ahead and of Suzanne. He decided to avoid her. It was quite easy to do. He worked on the third floor and she on the fourth.

He wondered how long it would be before he could face Suzanne again. Everything had seemed all right in the pub in Soho, but somehow now the thought of her hopeful, hurt face and of her mother's insidious comments was unbearable, and the problem of Devon raised its ugly head again. He wondered what Suzanne would have thought if she had seen him last night. And he wondered what her mother would have thought. He made himself some more Nescafé, looked at his watch and decided that he ought to be going.

Suzanne woke up on Monday morning with a sore throat, swollen glands and aching limbs. A touch of the 'flu. She wasn't sorry to stay at home. Work was all right but she was glad of an excuse not to see Nigel for a day or two.

Mrs Evans was delighted to have Suzanne at home. It gave her an opportunity to be alone with her. Have a few chats and give the girl some sound advice.

On Friday Suzanne went back to work, glad of a chance to escape from her mother's permanent nagging.

It was Thursday before Nigel realised that Suzanne was away. By then he felt strong enough to face her again and was beginning to think about Sunday dinner. He didn't really want to be alone on Sunday. Perhaps he would take Suzanne to a film in the evening. On Friday he and Suzanne lunched together in the staff canteen. Suzanne had an egg mayonnaise. Really nice egg mayonnaise in the staff canteen. Nigel suddenly realised that he was pleased to see her. Things seemed normal again.

For the next few weeks things went on much as they had done before. Nigel and Suzanne saw each other regularly. Nigel was put in charge of his department and enjoyed the importance of supervising the arrival of new stock. There was a new line in duvet covers for the summer. Bright whites and greens and cheerful pinks. The shop looked quite like a flower garden.

In the record department Suzanne sold an amazing number of singles of a song called 'Chiquitita' by Abba. She loved the song herself. In fact she had it on her brain for weeks . . . 'I'm a

66

shoulder you can lean on Chiquitita . . . .' There was something really comforting and meaningful about that song. It made her feel happy. Perhaps when summer came Nigel would think about Devon again. After all, Devon wasn't somewhere you would want to go to in the bad weather – now would you? She felt hopeful. Perhaps she would even dare to bring the subject up herself. Why not?

When she did tentatively mention Devon she and Nigel were having tea in the canteen. Her mouth was full of Mars bar. It was a Friday.

'Are you going down to see your parents in the summer?' she asked.

Nigel was stirring his tea, staring into the whirlpool formed by the spoon.

'Summer? What summer?' he said. He felt a wave of panic begin to swell inside him. He put down his spoon.

'In the summer,' she said. 'This summer. I should think Devon would be a nice place to visit in the summer. Nice to get out of London.'

'Nothing the matter with London,' he said.

'But Nigel, a change is always nice. I could come with you if you liked. I've never been to Devon.'

Nigel didn't know what to say. Everything had been so peaceful for the last few weeks and now the whole thing had started again. He gulped down his tea and scalded his throat.

'It's late,' he said. 'I've been sitting here too long. I must get back to work.' He stood up suddenly. 'See you on Monday,' he said.

Suzanne felt as if she had been slapped across the face. What was the matter with her? Was he so ashamed of her? Or was he ashamed of his parents? He was really weird. That was the truth of it. Any mention of Devon and he went all cold. All cold and unfriendly.

'Aren't you coming home on Sunday?' she called to his retreating figure.

He half-turned. 'Not this week, thanks,' he said and was gone.

Suzanne unwrapped another Mars bar.

Oh God, she thought, and began to hum to herself. 'I'm a shoulder you can lean on . . . Chiquitita . . . .'

When she went back to the record department after her tea break, her friend Mandy asked her if she had been crying.

Chapter VIII

Jack set off for the pub. The winter sunshine had not yet thawed the night's hard frost and the trees and hedgerows behind the village sparkled brightly. It was a Sunday, and as Jack walked, elated by the shining morning, he found himself thinking about his first wife. In fact he had noticed that these days he dwelt more and more frequently on the past. Only yesterday he had been remembering the fun he and his brother officers had all had in the mess in Lahore back in the late 'thirties. Of course the political situation had been difficult, not to say potentially dangerous in those days. But they'd had a good time all the same.

He'd liked the Indians, they were pleasant fellows on the whole – and ever so obliging. Of course the women were beautiful. The natives had a different point of view to the British, but that was hardly surprising when you came to think about it. There was a mess servant whom Jack had particularly liked. Damned good servant, too. He vaguely wondered what had happened to him – couldn't even remember the fellow's name after all these years – he wondered if he were still alive. Perhaps he'd been massacred in the Partition. A pity about Partition. Lahore was a lovely city. He supposed it must have changed a great deal over the years.

And now here he was today, thinking about Bobby. Everything would have been quite different if Bobby had lived. When she died he couldn't imagine life without her and now, nearly twenty years later, it was almost as though she had never existed. For a long time after he married Peggy, Jack hardly thought about Bobby, but these days he seemed to be thinking about her quite often. Of course she would have been old now, like him. He wondered how she would have aged. He chose to think that she would have been rather like Daphne Brown, with the same sort of faded prettiness. He supposed they would have retired to Suffolk, which was where Bobby's family came from. Bobby loved Suffolk. She had a brother who lived there, but he'd died shortly after her. Cancer too. The devil of a lot of bad luck ran in that family. Bobby and Jack had spent many a Christmas and Easter up in Suffolk with Bobby's brother and his family. In his mind's eye Jack suddenly saw Bobby standing on a chair with her arms stretched up, trying to put a sprig of holly behind a picture which hung over the fireplace in the sitting room. He could see her cherry red jersey and her lipstick which exactly matched her jersey. He wondered why on earth he could remember that so clearly. It didn't seem to be connected to any particular incident. He could even remember the picture. It was a reproduction of Constable's *Hay Wain*. Jack didn't feel sad with his memories, merely pleasantly nostalgic. The past was like a book you had once read or a film you had seen, existing only in the imagination. It didn't hurt.

Naturally life was different with Peggy. It was bound to be. Peggy was a completely different kettle of fish to Bobby. A lot of Jack's old friends had drifted away after he married Peggy. To be honest Bobby herself would not really have liked Peggy. And there was another matter to be considered. If Bobby had lived, there would have been no Josephine and Josephine was really what made his life worth living. Josephine was coming fifteen now and above all Jack hoped to live until she was grown-up. He wanted to see her settled with a good career, perhaps a husband, even a child. He loved the thought of a grandchild. No, Jack did not want to die yet – not so long as he could stay fit. Why should he when he enjoyed his quietly busy life and while there was Josephine's return from school to be looked forward to three times a year?

It was true that Peggy could be difficult at times – thoroughly tiresome, not to say madly irritating. But then Peggy was so much younger than he. The best attitude to adopt towards Peggy was to give her her head, he felt sure.

For the last year or so Peggy had been leading an increasingly independent life. She was often out – went to see her mother a great deal more than she used to. Even spent the night over at her mother's, sometimes as often as twice in one week. This meant that Jack had to look after the shop, which was not strictly speaking what he had bargained for. But he didn't really mind. If Peggy had a fault it was that she could be a little selfish at times and he was both surprised and pleased by her softening attitude towards her mother who really was getting on and who must be glad of the company.

By the time Jack reached the pub his hip had begun to play up a little. Damn nuisance, this hip of his. He could no longer do half the things he used to do. Couldn't even walk to the pub without the blasted thing playing up. Perhaps the cold air was bad for it.

'Morning, Major,' said the publican as soon as he saw Jack crossing the threshold. 'Lovely day.'

As a rule Jack stood by the bar with his pint, exchanging a friendly word with whoever turned up, but as his leg was bothering him he decided to sit down. He took out his pipe and was just lighting it when Colonel Willoughby from the Manor came in with one of his sons. It wasn't often that you saw Colonel Willoughby in the pub. He was a busy man, very tied up in local affairs. Jack was surprised when Colonel Willoughby and the boy came over to join him where he was sitting.

'Major Bennett,' said Colonel Willoughby, 'the very man I wanted to see. Do you mind if we join you? You know my boy, Julian?'

Jack struggled to his feet.

'Good morning,' he said. 'Please sit down.' He wondered what on earth Colonel Willoughby wanted to say to him.

The three of them talked for a while about the weather. It was very cold, but then anything was better than rain – perhaps they were in for a white Christmas. Only another two weeks until Christmas and the trouble with Christmas was that it had become so commercial these days. Colonel Willoughby didn't go near the shops much himself. He couldn't stand shopping and left it all to his wife but he was appalled by the amount of money she managed to spend on absolute rubbish at this time of year. With inflation going the way it was it would all be twice as expensive by next year. None of the news was very cheerful

71

these days either – more soldiers had been killed in Northern Ireland, and as for the American hostages, it was beginning to look as if they would never get out of Iran.

'We'd better drown our sorrows. Can I get you another?' Colonel Willoughby asked Jack.

When they had settled down to their second round of drinks Colonel Willoughby came to the point.

'I'll tell you what I wanted to ask you,' he said. 'I was thinking of your daughter, Joanna . . . .'

'Josephine,' Jack interrupted.

'Ah, yes, of course, Josephine. I hear she's a very competent girl – always helping in the shop and so forth – and I wondered if she would like a holiday job?'

'Good gracious me,' said Jack. 'She's not back from school yet, but I'll certainly ask her. What sort of a job had you in mind?'

'Well, it would take her a bit of time, but there's no hurry. My wife has been trying to sort out all the books at home – we want to get them catalogued. There must be nine or ten thousand books in the house. Could be even more. Some of them are quite rare. Anyway, my wife would like a bit of help. We were wondering if anyone around here would like to take it on, and then I thought of Joanna . . . .'

'Josephine.'

'So sorry – Josephine. How stupid of me. Do you think she would be interested?'

Jack was delighted by the suggestion. He knew perfectly well that Josephine was forever complaining to her mother that she didn't have enough pocket money. He also thought it would do her good to get out a bit and the Willoughbys were such nice people. Proper gentry. He glanced at the boy, Julian – a good-looking boy but he could have done with a hair-cut. Surprising his father putting up with that sort of thing.

'We've got the whole family coming down for Christmas,' said Colonel Willoughby, 'but if she's interested tell her to give my wife a ring at the end of the month. Well, we must be getting along. Come along, Julian, drink up.' The Colonel rose to his feet and nodded to Jack.

It was time for Jack to be getting home too. Peggy was out. Gone to see her mother for the day, but Jack had left a baked potato in the oven for his lunch. If he didn't hurry it would be spoiled.

That afternoon Jack settled down to do Peggy's accounts. He always did the accounts for her but he had been getting rather behind with them lately and this was a good opportunity to catch up. Mind you he preferred to do them when Peggy was out. If he did them with her around she kept butting in, looking over his shoulder and complaining that he was making mistakes which of course he wasn't. But by the time he had explained what he was doing and she had failed to listen, a great deal of time had been wasted. The accounts balanced which was just as well. There had been some trouble back in the summer. For one thing the till always seemed to be short. Peggy blamed Jack but quite frankly he had no idea what had been going wrong. Anyway, everything seemed to be in order now.

At five o'clock Jack began to expect Peggy back. By six she had not returned. She had taken the car and he sincerely hoped that she had not had an accident. She did not always pay attention when she was driving. If she wasn't back soon he would have to ring his mother-in-law but he decided to wait a little longer, so he settled down in an armchair beside the fire, his pipe neatly resting on an ashtray at his elbow, and began to read an excellent book on Napoleon's Egyptian expedition which he had just taken out of the library.

He was deeply engrossed in the Battle of the Pyramids, and wondering if he could add some Mameluke cavalrymen to his collection of soldiers when the telephone rang. As he rose to answer it his mind was still with the unsuspecting Napoleon who entered Cairo in the blistering July heat some eight days before the French fleet was annihilated by Nelson in Aboukir Bay. What strange and exciting times they had been.

Peggy's voice brought Jack back to the present.

'My mother's really rather poorly,' Peggy's voice shrieked down the telephone. Then she seemed to choke slightly – almost as though she were laughing. 'I think she'd rather like me to stop a while. In fact I think I'll stop overnight – ' another strangled choke. 'I wouldn't want to have an accident on the icy

73

roads, the roads are very icy you know. I'll be back by nine in the morning. If I'm not, just open the shop as usual – be a dear. Bye-bye for now, then.' The receiver was clanked back into place.

Half Jack's mind was still concentrating on Aboukir Bay. He tried to picture the French fleet – nine of their ships captured and the rest destroyed. He saw huge vessels floundering, holed and drawing water, their hulls turned up to the merciless Egyptian sun. He imagined Napoleon hearing the terrible news later in Cairo. Jack thought that Napoleon must have been about the same size as himself. He put his shoulders back and tucked his right hand into the front of his jacket. But something was nagging at the back of his mind. Was it something to do with Josephine? Josephine? No, of course not, he was being silly now. It was to do with Peggy. As he sat down and picked up his book it crossed his mind that Peggy had been lying. It had never occurred to him before that she might have been consistently lying for well over a year now. Oh dear, he supposed he couldn't really complain. She was a young woman still, and after all he didn't claim to be interested in all that sort of thing any more. He vaguely wondered who the fellow was and then turned his attention back to Egypt in 1799.

The following morning Jack was up early. By nine o'clock he had eaten and cleared away his breakfast. There was no sign of Peggy so he prepared to open the shop. At five to nine Mrs Chedzoy appeared.

'Mrs Bennett not well then?' she asked the Major.

'She's away,' said Jack. 'She spent the night with her mother.'

'I wouldn't wonder,' said Mrs Chedzoy darkly and darted away to fetch the broom. She came back and began to sweep round Jack's feet as he put his egg-cup back in the cupboard.

'She's been ever so good to her mother lately, has Mrs Bennett,' said Mrs Chedzoy. 'She must be that fond of her. But then your mother's always your mother.' The brush banged against the table legs. 'I can't think what she'll do when the poor dear passes on.'

Jack gave Mrs Chedzoy a steely glance and went away to open the shop.

74

Peggy turned up at half past ten. She looked tired and, Jack suddenly thought, old; not that he would dream of telling her that.

'I couldn't get the car to start,' said Peggy by way of an explanation. 'It's this cold weather. You're lucky to see me now. Could you just make me a cup of coffee dear, and I'll have an aspirin? I've a dreadful headache.' She flopped into a chair and lit a cigarette.

'How was your mother?' Jack asked.

'Fine,' said Peggy. 'It's not very comfortable sleeping on her sofa, I must say,' she added hastily.

'I don't know why you do it. I'm sure there's no need. Your mother has good neighbours who look in on her.'

Peggy scowled and inhaled deeply. Jack handed her a cup of Nescafé.

'There you are, dear. That should make you feel better. Why don't you go and lie down until your headache's better? I'll look after the shop.'

He didn't know where Peggy had been and he didn't particularly want to know. He was perfectly happy while she was away and he had no great desire for her company now that she was back. He supposed he should be hurt by her behaviour. But he wasn't really. He had long ago realised that he and Peggy advanced along parallel lines.

Peggy carelessly stubbed out her cigarette, leaving it smouldering in her saucer, and went upstairs to lie down. If Jack wanted to look after the shop he might as well do so. She kicked off her shoes and lay on the bed with her eyes closed. It seemed that the smallest amount of alcohol gave her a dreadful hangover these days. She wondered if it was something to do with her confounded age. But Bruce was only about a year older than she and he managed to put it back without much bother. It occurred to her that Bruce might no longer believe the lie she had told him about her age. She thought he believed her but she was terrified of him discovering the truth. As it was she had a nasty feeling that he wasn't quite so keen on her as he had been. She didn't like the way he'd chatted up the barmaid in that pub last night. You couldn't trust men, and she knew that lots of young girls went for the maturer sort of bloke. After all, Bruce was nice-looking with his thick grey hair and his tan. She dreaded to think what he must spend on that tan. She knew that if Bruce left her now she would have a problem finding somebody else. At fifty-four it might not be easy even with her figure. She was afraid of being alone – really afraid. She would rather have Jack for company than no one.

She dozed off and when she woke her headache had more or less gone. She found she was still thinking about Bruce. She and Bruce had had some good times together. Lucky Jack was so easy to fool. He believed everything she told him. As if she would ever dream of sleeping on her mother's sofa! Come to that, her mother wouldn't take kindly to the idea either. She wondered how she would manage when her mother died. The old girl couldn't last for ever.

Bruce didn't find it quite so easy to trick his wife, but things were made simpler by the fact that she had a fellow of her own and often spun a yarn about going off to visit some sick auntie. Then Bruce would give Peggy a ring and she would go and spend the night at his place. His daughter had moved out to live with her boyfriend, so that was no problem. Sometimes Peggy and Bruce would go off to the sea-side for a day to a beauty spot with a really nice, old-fashioned pub, and have scampi and Tartar sauce sitting up at the bar. Peggy loved scampi. They had even been to London for the night once. Peggy told Jack she was going to see Nigel. Heaven only knew what Bruce told his wife.

Peggy looked at her watch and saw that it was gone twelve. Oh God! She supposed she'd better be going downstairs. Jack was probably getting into a dreadful muddle in the Post Office. Josephine would be back next week. She could do a bit of work for a change.

For ten days Peggy heard nothing from Bruce, by which time she was feeling bad tempered and more than usually sorry for herself, so when Josephine came back from school she was surprisingly pleased to see her. It made a change. Peggy noticed that Josephine had grown taller since the summer and rather thinner. If she didn't have to wear those horrible spectacles she wouldn't be quite so bad-looking after all. Nobody could call Peggy vain but there was no doubt about it, she was a good-looking woman. It was there for all to see and it was a great shame that Josephine had not taken after her. All the same, the child had improved.

In a rare moment of maternal affection Peggy decided to take Josephine to buy some nice new clothes in Exeter. It would be good to get out and they might enjoy going round the shops together. Something trendy for Josephine for Christmas.

'Well, well, well, you girls going on a spree then?' Jack rubbed his hands together. He was thrilled to see Peggy taking an interest in her daughter at last. For years Josephine had been provided with second hand clothes from the annual village jumble sales.

No one was more surprised than Josephine by the unexpected turn of events. She had come home with her usual shining report with which she expected to delight her father, but from her mother she expected the indifference to which she had become accustomed.

Peggy's pleasure in her daughter soon waned. Shopping with the child was a nightmare and the Christmas crowds did nothing to improve the situation.

'How about this, dear?' Peggy elbowed two young women out of the way and took a slinky, low-cut gold number off the rail in C & A.

'Mummy, how could I wear that? I don't want to look like a prostitute.'

'Don't talk about prostitutes to me,' snapped Peggy to the amazement of a salesgirl who was standing by. 'Goodness me, I didn't know what a prostitute was at your age,' she went on in ringing tones.

Josephine wanted to say something along the lines of 'Well, you've certainly found out since,' but didn't dare. Instead she glared sullenly at her mother's skin-tight jeans and mock leopard-skin jacket. Tears of rage pricked her eyes.

'I thought you'd enjoy coming shopping with me,' said Peggy. 'Don't run away with the idea that you're doing me a favour. I've got plenty to do without dragging you all round the town and spending my hard-earned money on you. It's all very well for your rich school friends but you seem to forget that your father has retired. Money doesn't grow on trees, you know.'

Josephine was well aware that money didn't grow on trees.

'You've turned down the aubergine and the cerise, and now this.' Peggy shook the offending golden garment and replaced it angrily on the rail.

Josephine was deeply humiliated by her mother's behaviour, but she badly wanted some new clothes so she decided to humour Peggy.

'It's just that I'm not so pretty as you – or as thin – I'd be embarrassed to wear anything too bright. I'm sorry Mummy. I know it's awfully kind of you to take me shopping.'

Suddenly Peggy felt sorry for the child. Poor girl, it was hard luck. Peggy couldn't imagine what it would have been like to be less pretty than her mother. She had certainly never had that problem. People used to congratulate Mrs Baker on her beautiful daughter when Peggy was Josephine's age and Peggy secretly thought that her mother was rather jealous at the time.

Finally Josephine settled for a shapeless brown and green Indian dress. Delighted by the happy outcome – the dress was nice and cheap – Peggy even agreed to buy her a pair of black vinyl boots with heels. They were the most beautiful things Josephine had ever possessed.

At supper Josephine and Peggy were so cheerful that Jack could not have guessed at the traumas experienced in Exeter.

As they all sat eating their frozen peas and their pre-packed steak and kidney pie, Jack told Josephine of his encounter in the pub with Colonel Willoughby.

'How much do you think he'll pay me?' she asked, a greedy glint lighting up her eyes as she envisaged endless pairs of vinyl boots.

'I've no idea,' said Jack. 'Not very much I don't expect.'

'See to it that they pay the proper rate,' said Peggy. 'Or don't go there. I'm not having you taken advantage of. Besides, it'll be very inconvenient for me. I need you here to mind the shop.' Peggy got up to look for her cigarettes.

Jack winked at Josephine.

'You haven't been to see the soldiers since you came back,' he said. 'Not that there's much new. But I'm thinking of getting

78

some Mameluke cavalry and doing the Battle of the Pyramids.'

Josephine hadn't heard of the Battle of the Pyramids and neither was she sure what a Mameluke was. Her father was rather a baby when you came to think about it, going on about those soldiers. She used to love them – and she still quite liked them – but not in the same way. She remembered how real they had seemed to her on the night when she fell from the shed and broke her arm. She had been little then. Now she admitted secretly to herself that they were beginning to bore her rather. She would never tell her mother though.

But the job with the Willoughbys was quite another matter. That was full of promise. The holidays hadn't started too badly after all.

Chapter IX

Josephine was feeling rather pleased with herself. Christmas had come and gone peacefully enough and her mother had been away a good deal, leaving her in charge of the shop. She'd taken the opportunity to line her pockets. It was too easy. All you had to do was to wait until there were several people in the shop at once, and then, by mistake on purpose, you left the drawer of the till open so that you could take the next customer's money without ringing it up. That money went into your own pocket. No one could possibly ever find out. She'd done it all through the summer holidays with so much success that she'd been able to buy a really expensive fountain pen and some Mary Quant make-up. Not that she wore much make-up but she certainly felt that her new possessions had done something for her prestige at school. She pretended that the pen and the make-up had been given to her by a godmother who lived in Bolivia and who had turned up unexpectedly on a flying visit to Europe.

Josephine did not for one moment consider that she was stealing when she helped herself from the till. Her mother never paid her for looking after the shop, which was grossly unfair. Besides, her mother never gave her enough pocket money and it was no use pretending she couldn't afford to give her more. Anyone could see that Peggy spent pounds on herself, dyeing her hair, painting her nails and squeezing into the latest fashions. Josephine was only taking what was hers by right.

Now, feeling prosperous, and wearing her vinyl boots, Josephine was off to the Manor to help Mrs Willoughby catalogue the books. She'd taken care to explain that she could not go when her mother needed her in the shop – she had no desire to relinquish that source of income – but Mrs Willoughby was easy and more or less allowed Josephine to choose her own times.

Jack was glad for Josephine to have an occupation and sure that she would be helpful to Mrs Willoughby, but he rather missed her old enthusiasm for the soldiers. She still came and admired them but he sensed that she was beginning to outgrow them. Well, he supposed that that was fair enough.

Alone in the garage, he was concentrating on the Battle of the Pyramids. Napoleon had been a young man then and little knew what greatness lay ahead of him, and Jack wondered what Bonaparte's dreams had really been when he set out for Egypt. Although he knew it was a bit silly, when he was alone with his soldiers, Jack sometimes pretended that he was Napoleon. He stood reviewing the troops with his right hand tucked into his jacket, or he sat astride a white kitchen chair which he kept in the garage, threw his shoulders back, frowned, raised his right arm and pointed proudly ahead in imitation of David's well-known picture of Napoleon crossing the Alps. He was doing just that when he heard someone approaching across the garden. It was Mrs Chedzoy calling him to lunch. He stood up quickly. Mrs Chedzoy would think him very odd if she found him sitting like that.

'I'm on my way home now,' said Mrs Chedzoy. 'Mrs Bennett says your dinner's ready. Josephine phoned earlier, she's having hers up at Mrs Willoughby's.'

Jack rather wished that they didn't have to have regular meal times. It was all right when Josephine was there, but Peggy not only complained about having to prepare his food, but also refused to let him do it, with the result that meals alone with her had become more of a bind than a pleasure. He did not regard himself as an irritable man but at times he found it hard to countenance Peggy's uncivilised smoking habits and the inevitable recurrence of vanilla ice-cream for pudding. He had asked Peggy to use an ash-tray, but there never seemed to be one at hand and the ash was always dropped in the dirty plate or in the saucer of the coffee cup.

When Jack reached the kitchen, still brooding about ash-trays, he found Peggy in an unusually cheerful frame of mind. She had made some packet soup and there were sliced bread and Kraft cheese slices on the table.

'Cold outside,' said Jack shutting the back door behind him.

'Yes, I thought a nice bowl of soup would warm us up. There's a letter from Nigel which came this morning,' she handed the letter across the table to Jack. 'He wants to come down and stay. I must say it's high time he took the trouble to come and see his own mother. It must be five years since he last came here.'

'That will be nice,' said Jack as he glanced at the letter.

'Eat up your soup then, dear,' said Peggy.

'I see he's leaving his job,' Jack remarked. 'I wonder what he'll do.'

'Oh I expect he'll find something else quite easily. I mean he must have been fed up with all those sheets and towels and what not.'

Jack wondered how he'd stuck it for so long. After all, he wasn't a stupid boy, he'd surely find something more interesting to do now.

Was it really five years since Nigel stayed in Chadcombe? Of course Peggy had been to see the boy two or three times in London but Jack had only seen him once in all that time. He had been in London for a regimental get-together and had met Nigel for lunch the following day. A funny boy, Nigel, when you came to think about him. Very much one to keep himself to himself. Jack couldn't remember very much about his last visit but he seemed to think it had gone off all right. The boy had taken quite an interest in the soldiers, Jack thought. It would make a change to have him back. Liven the place up a bit.

'What I wonder,' said Peggy, 'is why he's not married yet. He's getting on you know. If he doesn't hurry up Josephine will be married before him. And I hope the Willoughbys are giving Josephine a proper lunch. I don't want that girl over-worked and half-starved.'

When Josephine came home later in the afternoon she reported that she had had an excellent lunch.

In fact she had thoroughly enjoyed her day. The Willoughbys had some wonderful books but no one had sorted them out for years. It was going to take ages to catalogue them all and to put them away in order. Mrs Willoughby was so kind and easy

82

to talk to and she had this sweet dog – a really gorgeous labrador. It was so sad, the old one had had to be put down about a year ago. Mrs Willoughby was really upset. They'd had a lovely lunch in the kitchen, and you should have seen their kitchen, it was huge with a great big, old fashioned dresser along one wall. It looked like something out of a film. Colonel Willoughby was there for lunch too. She felt quite shy of him but he was ever so nice. And this sweet dog was really funny the way he kept sitting by Mrs Willoughby hoping to get some food from her plate, but he wasn't allowed to be fed at meal times. They had pigeon pie for lunch and baked potatoes and Stilton and why couldn't the Bennetts have proper bread like the Willoughbys; that sliced stuff was just like rubber and you should have seen the piece of Stilton they had – it was huge – a whole half Stilton and this really sweet dog really likes Stilton – did you know that dogs liked cheese?

Peggy had never heard Josephine talk so much and she was glad she'd enjoyed her day, but she would put a stop to her going up there if she was going to start complaining about home. The Bennetts had always had sliced bread up to now, and Peggy saw no reason to change just because Mrs Willoughby didn't have sliced bread. It was all very well for Mrs Willoughby, she had plenty of money. And by the by, did she pay Josephine? No. Peggy thought as much. You could never trust the rich. How did you suppose that they got rich in the first place if it wasn't through cheating others?

Of course Mrs Willoughby would pay her. Josephine wasn't worried.

Peggy expected that pigeon pie and Stilton were all that Josephine would get for her trouble.

'And this really sweet dog kept wagging its tail . . .' Josephine went on. 'I wish we had a dog.'

Certainly not, they weren't having any dogs.

Josephine knew that already. They had gone through that several times. Jack had usually tried to take her side but Peggy was adamant.

What Josephine didn't tell her parents was that there was not only this really sweet dog, but also this terribly handsome boy.

She had spent the morning in the library with Mrs Willoughby until about twelve o'clock when they had gone into the kitchen. Mrs Willoughby put the pie which she had made earlier, and some potatoes, into the Aga. Josephine wondered why she put in so many potatoes but was too shy to ask. Then Mrs Willoughby offered Josephine a glass of sherry which Josephine accepted. She had never drunk alcohol before and she hadn't really liked it so she left her glass half full. In any case it made her feel slightly dizzy. She didn't tell her mother that, either. Then at about quarter past one Julian came into the library.

Perhaps Josephine had seen Julian once or twice in the shop, but somehow she could swear that she had never seen him in her life before. Neither had she ever seen anyone quite so extraordinarily wonderful. His presence made her acutely aware of herself and seemed at the same time to illuminate the room and electrify the atmosphere.

'What time's lunch?' Julian asked. He stood with all his weight on one leg, the other one nonchalantly bent at the knee.

'This is Josephine,' said Mrs Willoughby. 'She's helping me with the books.'

'Hullo.' Julian glanced for a moment in Josephine's direction. She blushed deeply and her voice failed to answer as he turned his heavy-lidded blue eyes back to his mother.

'So what time's lunch?'

Mrs Willoughby looked at her watch.

'Oh, any time now. Is your father in?'

'I dunno,' said Julian tossing his long, lank blonde hair out of his eyes.

'Well go and look for him and if he's in, come and tell me and we'll have lunch – it'll be ready now. You might just lay the table. There are four of us.'

'Okay.' Julian tossed his hair out of his eyes again and sauntered out of the room.

Josephine bent down to pick up a pile of books and to hide her confusion. She had seen supposedly handsome young men on television – pop stars whom her school-fellows worshipped – and she had seen what she and her mother called the 'yobs' in the village, but never in her entire life had she seen anyone, let alone a boy, who was so perfectly beautiful, so languid, so romantic, so magnificent as Julian.

At lunch his presence opposite her reduced her almost to silence. She wondered what he thought of her and tried desperately to please him with her winning ways. She sipped her cider most daintily and patted her mouth with her table napkin between each mouthful. She stared sensitively out of the window and stroked this really sweet dog whenever the opportunity presented itself, saying as she did so, 'Isn't he gorgeous?'

Julian, slouching nonchalantly in his chair, kept telling his father about some amazing speedboat that Peregrine's father was getting for their place in the Algarve. It was costing a bomb but Peregrine's parents were millionaires anyway so it was just like the Willoughbys buying a loaf of bread. Julian said that if he were really rich he'd get a helicopter – on the whole he thought it would be more fun than a private plane – after all you could just go to Exeter in it to do your shopping . . . .

Mrs Willoughby told him not to be silly and to clear the plates away. Colonel Willoughby merely scowled and remarked that if Julian wanted to make money he would have to learn about something called work and, judging by his 'O' level results, he hadn't even heard of it yet.

Julian knew an amazing number of people, like chairmen of ICI, managing directors of international companies, cabinet ministers, merchant bankers, judges and even heads of Oxford colleges who had never passed an exam in their lives. Not to mention Winston Churchill.

'You astound me,' Colonel Willoughby remarked and turned politely to ask Josephine – whom he called Joanna – about her school.

Julian put the Stilton on the table and addressed himself to his mother. It so happened that Julian had a friend who was a brilliant drummer and between them, if they only had the time, they could probably write a great musical. Julian's friend's father knew Andrew Lloyd-Webber so they would be bound to be able to get it put on in the West End.

Cynthia Willoughby was barely listening. She was wondering why she should mind being alone as her nearest and dearest entertained her with such nonsense when they came home. But she was not looking forward to Julian going back to school. He was her youngest child and the only one who still came home for any length of time. The house would feel empty again when term began. She glanced indulgently at Julian and said, 'Yes darling,' in a vague sort of way.

After lunch Julian announced that he had to mend something on his hi-fi.

'Bye Josephine,' he said and for an instant his cold blue eyes stared straight at her. He raised one eyebrow, flexed the muscles in his cheeks, tossed back his hair and was gone.

'Don't forget we're going to the Braithwaites this evening,' his mother called after him.

Josephine helped with the books for another hour or so, and was to go and help Mrs Willoughby again the following afternoon. Her whole life seemed suddenly to have changed. Never before had she felt so elated, rarely woken in the morning so intensely excited. When Julian said goodbye to her she realised that he had noticed her and probably found her deeply attractive – her fantasy knew no boundaries and she could barely wait for the afternoon. She decided to use her Mary Quant eye-liner and to leave her spectacles at home. This might make it rather difficult cataloguing the books. But she would manage. She thanked God for the vinyl boots.

After Nigel turned up the following afternoon Josephine was able to go to the Manor nearly every day until she had to go back to school. Nigel looked after the shop when Peggy wanted to go out. Josephine didn't see Julian again. But the job was not finished, and as Mrs Willoughby did not think that she could finish it alone, she asked Josephine to come back in the Easter holidays. So there was still hope.

Nigel's arrival caused quite a stir in the Bennett household. He came with a huge suitcase and announced that he would be staying for some time. He said that his being there would give Peggy and Jack the freedom to go out whenever they wanted. They wondered to what they owed this sudden change in his behaviour. After all, he had never shown any particular liking for the West Country in the past. He had only been to see them once since they had been at Chadcombe. And that was in the early days.

All that Nigel would say was that he had given up his job, was tired of London and needed a change. He hoped that Peggy and Jack didn't mind having him to stay for a while – until he found another job. He could pay for his keep – they needn't worry about that.

Peggy was quite pleased with the arrangement. She could do with the extra twenty pounds a week which Nigel gave her. She calculated that she could keep him for a good deal less than that. Besides, there was no end of errands he could run for her. Jack was getting so slow. It took him nearly half an hour to sell someone a jar of marmalade – by the time he'd found the right shelf and counted out the change. As for changing an electric plug – you might as well do it yourself as ask Jack. Nigel being there made it easier for Peggy to see Bruce. She could just slip out of an afternoon without even mentioning to Jack that she was going. As likely as not Jack wouldn't even notice – shut away in that garage.

Sometimes Nigel would go and talk to Jack in the garage, and Jack was not irritated by him. In fact since Nigel came there had been less ice-cream for lunch. He told his mother that it was the one thing he couldn't eat. In fact he was allergic to it. Jack supposed that he would eventually tire of cling peaches but in the meantime they made a welcome change.

Anyway Jack quite liked telling Nigel all about Napoleon's campaigns. Nigel hadn't even realised that Napoleon ever went to Egypt. Oh yes, Napoleon went to Egypt all right, although it could be said that he came home in rather a hurry. It was a long time since Jack had set up a battle other than a Napoleonic one. He had laid out Ramillies and Malplaquet in the past but he was gradually becoming exclusively interested in Napoleon. Even in his reading he found that he concentrated more and more on this one aspect of history which most intrigued him.

Nigel had unpleasant memories of the last stay at

Chadcombe and it had taken some time for him finally to make up his mind to come again. But Suzanne and her mother had become too much for him. He had had to get away. He had given up his job and his rented room and escaped to the West Country where he hoped to remain for a while before deciding what to do next. He put the disagreeable memory of his last visit out of his mind – it was several years ago now anyway – and decided to make the best of things. When he reached Chadcombe he was so relieved to be free of Suzanne that depsite the winter weather and the isolated surroundings he found it surprisingly agreeable.

Peggy and Josephine were out a great deal so he was left very much to his own devices, which suited him. Jack was all right, he kept himself to himself really, and Nigel enjoyed an occasional visit to the garage and quite enjoyed hearing Jack talk about his battles. He felt himself becoming more and more at ease with Jack and gradually began to confide in him as much as he had ever confided in anyone.

He told Jack that he had left London because he needed a change – he'd had enough of his job. But he also said that a woman was involved. He'd finished with her now. Jack asked no questions and Nigel left it at that.

In fact Jack was quite interested, since he had begun to wonder if the poor chap weren't a bit of a fairy. Not that he would have suggested anything of the sort to Peggy.

When the school holidays came to an end Mrs Willoughby gave Josephine twenty pounds. Thinking that this was hardly enough for all the trouble she had been to, Josephine helped herself to a nice leather-bound edition of *Tess of the D'Urbevilles* which she found high up on a shelf in the library among some old gazetteers. Mrs Willoughby certainly knew nothing of its existence and would never miss it. It would be far better to take that than to go through all the embarrassment of asking for more money. The only trouble was that it had a Willoughby book plate in it, so she would have to hide it carefully when she got home. There was no knowing what that nosey Nigel might make of it either.

Although Nigel's arrival left Josephine free to go to the Willoughbys', she rather resented his permanent presence in the house. He'd only been there for a week or so but whenever she wanted to go and see her father Nigel was there in the garage, usurping her place. So she hardly ever went there any more.

On the last night of the holidays she walked home with a heavy heart, clutching *Tess* tightly under her arm. More than half of January, the whole of February and nearly all of March before she would have a chance to see Julian again. She could think of nothing else. Even her secret hoard of money had become less interesting, except in so far as she would spend it on clothes in which she would attract Julian's attention at Easter.

'Back to school tomorrow?' said Nigel as she came into the shop.

'And when are you going to find yourself a job?' asked Josephine. 'You can't stay here for ever, you know.'

Nigel ignored the remark.

'Peggy rang to say she won't be home tonight. Granny's not very well. She's going to stay with her. She said to say goodbye in case she's not back before you go,' he said.

'How am I supposed to get to the station – walk?' Josephine yelled as she went through the back of the shop to the kitchen, slamming the door behind her.

Peggy had in fact left the car at home and gone to Exeter by bus which made Nigel think that his mother had never meant to come back that night. He briefly wondered what she got up to but as the thought of her was rather disagreeable he turned his mind to other things.

Back at school Josephine painted her face and boasted of her conquest of Julian Willoughby. She showed her amazed companions the copy of *Tess* which he had stolen from his father's library to give her and in which she had written on the fly-leaf in disguised, crooked writing, 'For my own darling Josephine from your devoted friend and lover J. W.'

Her school-fellows began to regard her in a different light although there was something pretty fishy about the whole thing. And – if he loved her so much – where were the fat letters which ought to be arriving by every post? Josephine thought that perhaps she might have to write a few to herself.

89

Miss Hadley, the Latin teacher, was at a loss to understand Josephine's below standard work that term. She would even have gone so far as to say that she had misjudged the child.

Chapter X

Six months later Nigel was still at Chadcombe. He had, without success, applied for one or two jobs locally, and had made it plain to Peggy and Jack that he had no intention of returning to London in the immediate future. To a certain extent he took over the running of the shop. It did not take him long to realise that Peggy's management was both slipshod and wasteful – all this to-ing and fro-ing to Exeter for one item from the supermarket which was then sold at little or no profit to a favoured villager. No wonder she was getting deeper and deeper into financial trouble. Besides, she had a habit of running out of basic essentials and custom was beginning to drop off.

Peggy was perfectly happy to leave the shop in Nigel's hands and rather relieved by his efficient re-organisation. Her overdraft was something which she had been putting off thinking about. Now she had a feeling that it would look after itself. But she wanted to know what a young fellow like Nigel was doing burying himself in the country. He didn't seem to have any friends and had cut himself off from London completely. A few letters came for him in the early days – all addressed in the same small, neat handwriting and post-marked 'Cricklewood'. Peggy had tried to find out who they were from but to no avail. Nigel was very uncommunicative.

Although Nigel was a help, Peggy wasn't sure she wanted him around indefinitely. For one thing she didn't like him much. But then she wasn't sure that she was going to be around indefinitely herself. Quite frankly she'd had enough of being shut up in that shop all day and she had other plans.

Peggy had gone for a drink with Bruce in the Smugglers' Arms – a nice pub they'd found out in the country. Peggy was having a Bacardi and lime. Bruce was on his second pint.

91

'You want to watch your waistline.' Peggy patted Bruce's stomach which seemed to be nearly bursting the buttons off his nice new pink shirt.

Bruce grunted and drained his drink. He put down the glass and wiped his mouth with the back of his hand.

'Have the other half?' he said, pointing at Peggy's glass.

'I don't mind if I do.'

While Bruce was fetching the drinks Peggy sat thinking and gazing at the back of her outstretched hand. She wasn't sure about her new nail-varnish.

When Bruce came back she took out a cigarette and pushed the packet across the table to him.

Bruce lit their cigarettes and sighed.

'Well, well, well,' he said.

'Why don't we just go away together?' said Peggy suddenly. She felt that their relationship needed a jolt. Bruce wasn't quite his old self these days. Not exactly moody, but quieter than he used to be. For some time she had been waiting for him to make a move. They couldn't go on the way they were for ever. But she'd waited long enough and the time had come for her to say something.

'That would be out of the question,' said Bruce. After all, he had a wife and there was Jack to be considered – and Josephine, come to that. Of one thing Bruce was certain: he didn't want to be saddled with Josephine.

'Look, love,' said Peggy, 'I've told you before, I married Jack when I was alone. I had no one else to turn to. It was a bad time in my life. I never stopped to think how boring he was. Anyway, how was I to know he was going to spend the rest of his life playing with toy soldiers? It amounts to mental cruelty.'

'But the poor bugger's been quite good to you – '

'Good? He's done nothing for me which didn't suit him. He only thinks of himself from morning to night. Don't you want us to go away? We could go abroad – Spain – somewhere nice and warm – run a hotel.'

'We wouldn't have any money.'

'The shop belongs to me,' said Peggy. 'I could sell that. Jack wouldn't want the shop – not if he was on his own.'

'What about Josephine?' Bruce didn't really want to know

about Josephine.

'Oh Josephine. She hasn't got much longer at school. She'll be grown-up soon. She'll look after Jack. She's always preferred her father.'

'Look Peggy, love,' said Bruce, taking her hand and gazing sincerely into her eyes. 'You and me – we've had a bit of fun – right? But no way can we start running away to Spain. No way.'

Peggy pouted.

'You don't love me,' she said.

'You know that's not true,' said Bruce, 'but let's look at it this way – I've got this situation. You know I have. Well, to be honest I've got these two situations. There's the wife,' he pointed at a spot on the table, 'and there's the business,' he pointed at another spot.

'Oh go on,' said Peggy, 'you're just making excuses. What is there for us here? You haven't got anything going with your wife and as for Jack – I've told you, there's been nothing of that sort of thing for years now –'

'It's not just that, Peggy.' Bruce leaned towards her and smoothed her cheek with his knuckles. 'I mean you know I'd love to live with you, but I can't just run out on my family . . . .'

Peggy was furious. She could barely control her temper, but somehow she managed to hold her tongue. She hoped Bruce needn't think he could just run out on her either. She opened her new white bag – it was ever such a nice bag – took out some lipstick and powder and carefully adjusted her make-up. She wondered what her next move should be. She thought Bruce was just being cautious. Like most men, he couldn't make decisions. She'd had enough of shilly-shallying and she would surely win him round in time. He certainly didn't owe any loyalty to that slut of a wife of his. It was going to be more difficult than she had bargained for but she felt certain that it would be all right in the end. She put away her make-up and squeezed Bruce's thigh under the table.

'Let's have another drink,' she said. 'We'll talk about us another day.'

When Peggy reached home she was in no mood to be crossed. Nigel was watching the television and Jack had gone to

93

bed. What a dull lot they were. Nigel just sat there not saying anything. Unfriendly sort of beggar. You'd think he might want to confide in his own mother. Forty-eight hours she'd been in labour, and never so much as a 'thank you'. It hadn't been so bad with Josephine. You had to give the child that.

'Time you found yourself a girl,' she said sharply. 'What are you now? Thirty-four, thirty-five? Good heavens, at your age you should be running around having a good time. You won't be young for ever, you know.'

Nigel stood up, switched off the television and made to leave the room.

'Well you're certainly not like your father,' Peggy went on. 'Not at all. He had his faults, but at least he was a real man. It was twice a night with him and three times on Saturdays – enough to tire anybody out,' she said to Nigel's retreating back. What on earth was the matter with the boy?

The next morning there was a letter for Jack. Peggy was grumpily laying the breakfast when the post arrived. Jack was making the toast.

'It's from Daphne Brown,' he said, looking at the envelope. He hadn't heard from the Browns for some time.

'Oh dear, oh dear. What sad news.'

'Jack – the toast – it's burning!' Peggy pushed her husband unceremoniously to one side and snatched the toast from the grill.

'Can't you look what you're doing?' she said. 'It's not very difficult – to make the toast without burning it.'

'Maurice Brown's dead,' said Jack.

'That's no excuse for burning the toast,' said Peggy.

Jack looked at Peggy. He sometimes wondered if she were mad. Was it not a form of madness to be so totally selfish? He need never have married her. Perhaps marrying her was the only serious mistake of his life – but he didn't care to dwell on that. He preferred to make a quiet life for himself and to block out the unpleasantness. If he dwelt on the unpleasantness, it might destroy him. There were plenty of things to be optimistic about – he must dwell on them. For years now he had been satisfactorily building a little world around himself. It was the only thing to do.

94

'Peggy,' he said, 'Maurice Brown is dead.'

'I heard you the first time, dear.'

Jack had not seen the Browns for some time; not since they had come to lunch over a year ago on their way down to Torquay. It had been a pleasant occasion and Peggy had behaved surprisingly well, producing a meal that was above her usual sloppy standard, but he had heard from Daphne at Christmas and knew that Maurice's condition was rapidly worsening. Nevertheless he was shocked and saddened by the news of his friend's death. Daphne wrote to say that the funeral had already taken place, it was a quiet affair for the family only. The clergyman had said some very nice things about Maurice. Of course Daphne realised that life, for Maurice, had become a burden and so for his sake, she should be glad, but she had been privileged to be married to him for over fifty years and she found it almost impossible to accept that he was no longer there. Her children had been wonderful, a great support in every way, but they had their own lives to lead. If there was any chance of seeing Jack and Peggy, Daphne would be delighted. Perhaps they could get away from the shop for a day or two and come up and stay. The garden was looking lovely and they might do a little sight-seeing. She wondered if the Bennetts had ever visited the Abbey at St Albans, or the Roman theatre. Or she could take them to Hatfield or Knebworth, both of which lovely houses were nearby.

Peggy clattered around making toast and dropping ash all over the kitchen as Jack read his letter. Jack supposed that she would have little desire to visit Hatfield, or St Albans Abbey for that matter, but he was tempted by the idea. Perhaps they might cheer Daphne up a little.

'Do you think we could leave Nigel in charge of the shop and go and stay with Daphne for a couple of days?' he suggested.

'I should hardly think she'd welcome us, pushing ourselves in where we're not wanted,' snapped Peggy. 'The poor woman's just been widowed.'

'Precisely,' said Jack, 'and she's written to ask us to stay.'

'You go if you want to, then. But don't expect me to come. I'm far too busy. You seem to forget that I have the shop to run. It's no use leaving it to Nigel. He never does anything

95

properly. It's time that boy got himself a job. Then he would learn what work was really like.'

Jack decided to visit Daphne without Peggy. He would be glad to get away for a few days and as Daphne must be feeling very much alone at the moment perhaps he could be of some comfort to her. Deep inside he felt the faint murmur of a thrill at the prospect of spending a day or two alone with Daphne. She reminded him in a way of Bobby, so that somehow her presence transported him back into the past and made him feel young again. Besides she emanated an aura of peace, stability and order, all of which seemed to be lacking at Chadcombe.

'Well, we'll get a bit of peace and quiet with you away,' said Peggy.

Jack stared at her with blank incomprehension.

'Yes, I suppose you will,' he replied as he made to leave the kitchen.

'Where are you off to, then?' Peggy asked.

'I'm going to the garage.'

'Well that's a fine thing,' said Peggy. 'Don't bother to ask me if I want any help, will you? There's a case of baked beans in there needs unpacking.' She waved a hand towards the door into the shop.

'I'll leave you to do that in peace and quiet.' Jack closed the back door and made his way up the garden. He didn't often answer Peggy back, it wasn't worth it. But he was upset and felt provoked by her callous reaction to Maurice Brown's death. He supposed she would dance on his grave when he finally passed on. Why in God's name had he ever married her? he wondered. He must have been mad. He cast his mind back to the early days of his widowhood. Sex and company, he thought. What a fool he'd been. How could he have ever been attracted to Peggy? She was not really his type. She was so common. Anyway he wasn't interested in sex nowadays – hadn't been for a long time – and besides he preferred to be alone. Well, well, well, he'd made his bed . . . as the saying goes. He reached the garage door and his thoughts turned to Josephine. Of course if he had never married Peggy, there would have been no Josephine. So it was worth it all in the end.

Peggy scowled through the window at Jack's retreating back,

96

then lit a cigarette and sat down disconsolately to another cup of coffee.

Just as she was finishing it, Nigel put in an appearance. He looked unshaven and smelt faintly of sweat. Peggy glowered at him. He was, she thought, intensely irritating. She watched him mix a cup of Nescafé and put a piece of sliced bread under the grill. Neither of them had spoken since he came into the room. Peggy wondered what she had done to deserve such a dull husband, such a wet son and such a plain daughter.

Nigel stood with his back to her. He was bending slightly, his hands on his knees, watching his toast lest it burn.

So concerned about his bloody toast, thought Peggy.

Finally Nigel turned his toast and settled back in the same bent position to watch the second side.

'You can go to the cash-and-carry this morning,' said Peggy. 'We need tea, frozen peas – various other things. I'll give you a list.' She couldn't wait to be rid of Nigel. All he ever did was to look after number one.

When Nigel had finally gone, Peggy was left alone – Josephine was still at school. She was obliged to unpack the case of baked beans herself, which filled her with resentment. You'd have thought that with two men about the place one of them could have done it for her. And there was no Mrs Chedzoy that morning either. Then Peggy's thoughts turned to the freedom she would have when Jack went away. She was looking forward to telling Bruce the good news. Perhaps Bruce and she could go away somewhere – the Caribbean. Wouldn't she just love to go to the Caribbean – all those Bacardis and palm trees – well, of course they wouldn't be able to afford to go there, that was just a daydream, but perhaps they could go to the Costa Brava – or even Capri. If only they could get away for a few days to somewhere nice and romantic she was sure she could work on Bruce and persuade him to leave that lousy wife of his and go away with her for good. She was convinced it would work. She began to stack the baked beans away more cheerfully, suddenly careless of her present drudgery.

The shop was quite busy and full of chat that morning. Mrs Willoughby came in for some soap powder and asked when Josephine would be back. They hadn't finished cataloguing all

97

the books. The publican's wife came in to look for a birthday card for her niece and several of the villagers came for their weekly order. Only those without cars shopped regularly in Chadcombe. The others went to Exeter. The village was rife with gossip at the moment because two wives from the cottages at the lower end of the village had done a 'midnight flit' together. There had always been something a bit queer about those two.

Peggy was full of the drama at lunchtime, so that her irritation with Jack and Nigel faded into the background as she regaled them with the latest scandal. It seemed to have all begun when the two women went blackberrying together in the autumn. Peggy was particularly sorry for the abandoned husbands and the children – both women had children – and as for the two women she thought they were perfectly disgusting. If they ever came back to the village she for one wouldn't be able to bring herself to speak to them. Now, she thought, she'd heard it all.

Jack was always mildly surprised by the number of dramas which shook so small a community as Chadcombe. Only a year ago a married woman and mother of three had got drunk in the pub and done a striptease in the bar. There had been a dreadful kerfuffle at the time. Peggy heard all the news in the shop, and as far as Jack was concerned the more scandals the better because Peggy was a happier person and far easier to live with when she was immersed in one of the village sagas.

After lunch Jack went off to change his library book. He never liked to miss the library van, and besides he had ordered a new book on Napoleon which he hoped they would have for him by today. Peggy told Nigel to look after the shop as she needed a bit of fresh air. In fact she wanted to go and look at the cottages from which the two women had eloped. Not that she expected to see anything. On her way back she would ring Bruce from the call box. She couldn't bear the thought of that nosey Nigel minding her business. As it happened Bruce was out, teaching someone to drive she presumed, so she left a message for him on his answer-phone. She was longing to tell him that Jack was going away and to see what he thought about going to Spain.

Jack was not altogether surprised by Peggy's enthusiastic response to his planned departure. He knew perfectly well that she had someone up her sleeve, but to be perfectly honest he didn't care. Occasionally he mildly wondered who the fellow was, but he was wise enough to know that the truth would only infuriate and disgust him were he to discover it, so he made no efforts in that direction. In any case he was really looking forward to his visit to St Albans. He wrote to Daphne to commiserate over Maurice's death and at the same time proposed himself for three or four days in the middle of July. He thought he could combine his visit with fetching Josephine from school, as he had done the time before.

Bruce had had a sod of a day. He'd started the morning with a puncture, then two of his pupils had failed their driving tests and were badgering him for more lessons and he had no idea how he was going to fit them in, then a middle-aged woman had nearly run over a child on a zebra crossing. A seventeen-year old school girl had slapped his face when she got out of the car, and told him that she would take her custom elsewhere. All he had done was to put his hand on her knee, well all right – her thigh, to help her with her clutch control. Anyway it was all her own fault. What did she expect if she went around half-naked in that T-shirt and the shortest skirt you'd ever seen. Then when he finally got home, tired and fed up, he found a note on the kitchen table from his wife, which read, 'Gone to the cinema. Back late. Don't wait up. See you. Judy.' He didn't believe a word about the cinema. He turned on his answer-phone and was quite glad to hear that Peggy had been trying to get in touch. He'd give her a ring and see if she could come round and cheer him up.

When Peggy arrived she was full of the joys of spring. Of course Judy hadn't gone to the cinema. She was off with that bloke of hers. Bruce knew by now what a liar she was.

'Well let's make the best of it,' said Bruce, sliding his arm round Peggy's shoulder.

Peggy told him about Jack going away.

'Let's have a fling,' she said. 'Nigel can look after the shop. He won't say anything to Jack.'

Suddenly Bruce felt that he too would like to get away.

99

'Why not,' he said. 'After all we're not getting any younger, you and I.' He kissed her ageing neck.

'Oh go on,' said Peggy, pushing him gently away. 'Let's have a g. and t. to celebrate first.' Things were really going her way.

Bruce fetched the gins and tonics and sank into the sofa beside Peggy.

'Where shall we go?' he asked.

Chapter XI

Peggy was thrilled by her plans to go on holiday with Bruce. Life was certainly looking up for a change. She spent an afternoon going round all the travel agents in Exeter and came home with a mountain of gaudy brochures which she hid under her bed, away from prying eyes.

As soon as Jack went off to the garage or the pub, she brought them out and spread them over the counterpane. It was agony deciding where to go. Venice looked nice with those gondolas but she didn't fancy too much sight-seeing. She'd seen enough sights when she went on that cruise with Jack after he retired. Not that she didn't enjoy the cruise – all that sunshine and cheap wine, and she still treasured some of the souvenirs she'd brought back – but to be honest sight-seeing was not really her thing. What she needed was a rest.

She spent hours going through all the brochures before finally reaching a decision. Bruce had told her to choose. He was easy.

When she had at last settled for the Hotel El Cid in a recently developed resort on the Costa del Sol, she met Bruce for a drink to discuss it.

The Hotel looked gorgeous from the brochure – with its two swimming pools, its sun terraces, its Don Quixote bar and its 'English Pub'. There was a t.v. room with English-language videos on request, hairdressers and souvenir shops were on the premises, and there was a nightly flamenco show in one of the bars.

Bruce agreed that that was just what they both needed to cheer them up – give them a lift as it were. As far as he was concerned he'd just about had enough. He didn't feel old, not he, but he had begun to worry lately about the future. Age was all in the mind, he knew that, but after all, he was in his mid-fifties now and he didn't want to waste time. Peggy and he had every right to enjoy themselves. They did enough for other people most of the time and, to be perfectly frank, what had they ever got for their efforts?

Peggy agreed with everything Bruce said. She thought that if you didn't do things when you had the chance, then life would pass you by.

The next day Peggy was off to Exeter again to book the tickets and to buy a few things which she would be needing for the holiday. She found a gorgeous claret-coloured nylon negligé and matching nightdress in C & A. Ever so lacy. Well you couldn't let a man take you on holiday without making a bit of an effort for him could you?

Much against her will Peggy was forced to admit that at the age of fifty-five even she would be better advised to avoid wearing a bikini. In any case one-piece suits were coming right into fashion again. She bought a black and white one with a deeply plunging back and a halter neck. She really did have something to look forward to at last. What a pity they couldn't go away for longer. But still you had to count your blessings, and you might say that it was lucky old Maurice Brown popped off when he did. There was only another week to wait and then she would be away.

When she had finished shopping Peggy decided to look in on her mother. She had been rather forgetful about Mrs Baker lately and perhaps the poor thing would be wondering what had happened to her.

It seemed to Peggy that her mother took an age to come to the door, and when she finally opened it, Peggy was quite shocked by the sight of the old lady. She looked bony, wizened and transparent. She seemed to have shrunk away to nothing and to be less steady than usual on her feet. For a moment Peggy forgot about her black and white bathing suit and her claret negligé.

'Good Lord alive!' she exclaimed. 'Are you all right? You look like death warmed up. For heaven's sake sit down.' Peggy dropped her parcels inside the front door and helped her mother into the sitting room.

As Mrs Baker sat down she was convulsed by a spasm of

coughing so violent that Peggy thought she might die. She seemed to be about to choke and tears streamed down her papery cheeks.

Peggy was frightened. She had no idea what to do. If she hit her mother on the back the poor thing would surely collapse. There was a nasty rattle in the old lady's chest and she looked as if she hadn't eaten for a month. Peggy rushed to the kitchen for a glass of water which she stood holding helplessly towards her mother as Mrs Baker tried to collect herself. When she finally stopped coughing a dreadful whistling sound rose from her throat and she seemed to have difficulty in breathing. At last, with a weary look on her face, she leaned back in her chair able to breathe freely.

'Bronchitis,' she whispered faintly. 'It'll probably kill me off when the winter comes.'

As long as it didn't kill her off now, Peggy thought, and prevent her from going away. That would be just her luck.

'Oh come on,' said Peggy. 'You're as fit as a fiddle. You're not going to die yet.'

Mrs Baker wished that every day would be her last.

'There's not much point,' she told Peggy, 'in sitting here day in and day out, feeling cold and tired and lonely. I can hardly see and I daren't go out any more. My neighbour does a bit of shopping for me, but when you come to think of it I'm only a trouble to her. Mind you, she's very good to me.' Mrs Baker began to cough again but this time the spasm lasted less long.

'If I talk or move, the coughing comes on again,' she spluttered.

'Let me get you a nice cup of tea,' Peggy suggested.

'That would be good of you, dear.'

When Peggy brought the tea through from the kitchen she found that her mother had dozed off. She shook her gently by the shoulder and was horrified by the frailty of the old lady's frame.

'Wake up, dear. Here's your tea.'

Mrs Baker stretched out a trembling hand and took the flowery cup which her daughter held out towards her.

'You should call a doctor,' said Peggy.

'What can the doctor do?' Mrs Baker wanted to know.

103

'Give you some tablets for that nasty cough of yours.'

'I don't want any tablets. Get the doctor round here and all he'll try to do is to keep me alive. When you reach my age and you have nothing to live for, you're better off dead.'

'What do you mean – nothing to live for?' Peggy wanted to know. She was upset by her mother's attitude and wasn't sure how to answer her. 'You've got a nice house, friends and neighbours. And there's me and Josephine. And even Nigel. You like seeing Nigel, don't you?'

Mrs Baker gave a snort which merely served to set her off on another bout of coughing.

'Why didn't you let me know you were ill?' Peggy asked when the coughing eventually stopped.

'I didn't want to bother you,' said Mrs Baker. 'You're always so busy.'

Peggy looked at her watch. She ought to hurry if she was going to catch her bus, but she was for once quite worried about leaving her mother. Oh well, she'd come back again before she left for Spain. And it wouldn't be long before Josephine came home. Josephine could come and spend a few nights with her grandmother and keep an eye on her. It would do the child good to think of somebody else for a change.

'Well Mum,' said Peggy, 'I'll clear away the tea-cups and then I'll be on my way. Mustn't miss the bus.'

She hurriedly washed the tea things, then put her head round the sitting-room door, said cheerily, 'Bye-bye then. Look after yourself,' and was gone.

The next morning Peggy was in the shop when the telephone rang.

'Mrs Bennett?'

'Yes, speaking,' said Peggy.

'You don't know me, I'm Mrs Connell. I live next door to your mother, Mrs Baker – '

'What's happened?' Peggy was worried. If her mother had died she might just be buried in time for Peggy to leave for Spain.

'Well, it's like this,' Mrs Connell went on, 'I've been looking in to see your mother regularly. I've done a bit of shopping for her – you know it's not always easy for old people to get out and about – '

Peggy wished the woman would get on with what she had to say. Of course if Mrs Baker had died, Peggy would need a break after the funeral – she'd need to get over the shock –

'Well, I looked in to see her this morning,' said Mrs Connell, 'it must have been about nine fifteen – no, I think it was half past nine because the milkman doesn't come till then and the milk was on the doorstep as I set out. I remember stopping to take it in. Well, then I went round to Mrs Baker's – I've got a key to her door. She gave it to me a while back. You know it saved her the trouble of coming to let me in. She had slowed down a great deal, poor dear. Now Mrs Bennett, I don't want to upset you, but she wasn't at all well when I looked in this morning.'

Peggy caught her breath in relief.

'Thank God she's all right!' she exclaimed.

But Mrs Connell didn't think that Mrs Baker was really all right.

'To tell you the truth,' she said, 'when I first saw her, I had the fright of my life. I thought the dear lady had passed on. All blue she was. Just sitting in the armchair, staring straight ahead of her. I don't think she'd been to bed all night. Quite vacant, she looked. I said to her, "Mrs Baker dear, are you all right?" Well, when she heard my voice, she turned her head in my direction. I'll tell you, Mrs Bennett, I've never been so relieved in all my life. Naturally I called the doctor. He's very good, Dr Jones. He came straight round and when he saw your mother he said she should be in hospital. I must say, that's just what I thought myself. She couldn't be left alone. Not in that condition. Anyway Dr Jones called an ambulance and they took Mrs Baker off to hospital about half an hour ago. The doctor asked me to let you know . . . .'

It seemed that Mrs Connell would never stop talking, but at last she said goodbye. Peggy put down the telephone, went into the kitchen and lit a cigarette before calling to Nigel who was reading the paper in his bedroom.

When Peggy told Nigel what had happened, he was quite upset. He felt faintly guilty about the fact that he hadn't visited his grandmother for some time. He liked her in a detached sort

105

of way. She was quite unlike his mother, more open and less selfish. She had nothing much to say to him, nor he to her, yet he had a faint feeling of affinity with her. He saw them both as unwanted by the Bennetts and unwanted by society. He could well imagine sitting alone, with no aim or future in view – living in a sort of void. After all, he did feel as though he lived in a void, although he took quite an interest in the shop. All the same it seemed at times as though nothing touched him and he affected nothing. That was why he did those silly things – well he'd kept himself quite well under control for some time now, but he was still occasionally tempted.

That afternoon Jack looked after the shop while Nigel drove Peggy to visit Mrs Baker in hospital. Mrs Baker was lying in bed gazing dully ahead and when they arrived she showed no awareness of their presence. Nigel leaned over the bed and spoke to her but she still did not react. Peggy was all upset, it frightened her to see her mother like that. Mrs Baker's hair, her face and nightdress were all as white as the pillows against which she lay. Even the walls of the ward were white. Her pale, watery blue eyes remained expressionless and her thin white hands lay motionless beside her.

After a while Nigel and Peggy decided that their presence was quite unneeded and they slipped quietly away.

'She looks as if she's waiting for something,' Nigel remarked on the way home in the car. 'I suppose she's just been waiting to die for a long time now.'

Peggy looked daggers at Nigel. Waiting to die! Did you ever? The boy needed his head examining.

'If you ask me,' said Peggy, 'she's past thinking about anything, the poor dear.' She started to snivel. 'She mustn't die. I can't bear it if she dies,' she went on. 'She's such a lovely person. I don't know what I'd do without her . . . .'

'You'd have to find another lie to tell about where you spend Thursday nights,' said Nigel with sudden venom.

If they had not been in the car Peggy would have slapped Nigel's face. How dared he talk to his mother like that. She, Peggy, had always treated her mother with the utmost respect as Nigel could see. Times had certainly changed since her young day. She would never have dreamed of cheeking Mrs

Baker in that way. At the mention of her mother, Peggy dissolved into tears. Nigel was just hard-hearted, talking about death in that callous way.

When they reached home Jack had made a pot of tea to welcome them. He was quite surprised by the extent to which Peggy appeared to be upset about her mother. Poor Peggy. Perhaps he had been misjudging her all the while and she was not so unfeeling as he had thought.

Nigel returned to see his grandmother the following day. Peggy was too distressed to go back to the hospital and in any case she couldn't see the point if Mrs Baker didn't even recognise her. Jack said he would go the next day. He hadn't seen his mother-in-law for some time, but he thought she might be lonely in hospital and even if she didn't speak she might be taking things in. It would be terrible to abandon her at a time like this.

Three days after going to hospital Mrs Baker died. She died peacefully according to the nurses and without ever having shown any sign of awareness.

Peggy could not believe her ears when she heard what had happened. She was going to sue the nurses, the doctor, the hospital, the health service. It was a disgrace. There had been absolutely nothing wrong with her mother. She could have lived happily for another ten years or so. Peggy wanted to know what the country was coming to. She supposed it was something to do with government cuts. You would have thought that with a woman for Prime Minister that sort of thing wouldn't happen. Hadn't Mrs Thatcher ever heard of Florence Nightingale? Peggy would never have voted for her if she thought it would come to this. She went on and on and on.

Jack was quite unable to understand her attitude. She had never been very close to her mother and Mrs Baker, who was old, frail, tired and probably lonely, had died peacefully. It was natural for Peggy to feel a sense of loss at her mother's death, but what she was saying appeared to bear no relation to anything.

The funeral was arranged to take place five days later so Jack was obliged to telephone Daphne and postpone his visit. Josephine would come home a few days before the end of term so as to be there.

'It's one thing after another,' said Peggy. 'First Maurice Brown and now my mother. I'll somehow have to find time to get into Exeter and buy a hat for the funeral.'

When Peggy met Bruce for a drink that evening she was in despair. As she had said to Jack, it was one thing after another. How selfish of her mother to have died when she did. She could have died at any other time and no one would have minded. Peggy had been back to the travel agent. There was no chance of changing the booking. It was already July and the holiday season was in full swing. There was not a room to be had on the whole Spanish coast. Would you believe your luck?

Bruce was half-sorry and half-relieved. One way and another the holiday would have produced a great many complications at that time, but he promised Peggy faithfully that before the year was out they would go away together. They'd wangle it somehow. Make it a week. The four days they'd planned would hardly have been long enough.

On the day of the funeral it was drizzling and Peggy was crying as they arrived at the crematorium, and she cried again as the coffin was finally pushed out of sight. Her poor old mother, she would miss her in a way, and to think that she might have been on the Costa del Sol at that very moment with the sun shining, lying on the beach and getting brown.

Of course it crossed Peggy's mind that with the bit of money she would inherit from Mrs Baker, she and Bruce might be able to afford to go to the Caribbean during the winter. Some of those winter excursions were surprisingly reasonable. She would arrange it somehow, even if it involved Jack guessing what was going on. She could always say that she was going with her friend June, the hairdresser. June had given her an alibi often enough before.

When Peggy discovered that her mother's possessions had been left equally between Josephine and Nigel, she was absolutely furious.

What had they ever done – either of them – to deserve anything? Fancy disinheriting your own flesh and blood. Peggy knew that her mother was a selfish old woman but she never imagined that she would go to those lengths.

As far as Jack could see, Mrs Baker was very wise. It would be nice for Nigel and Josephine to have a little something of their own and after all Peggy was all right. She didn't need anything. The shop was hers, Jack had put it in her name when he bought it. Besides he had a small life insurance policy and although she would never be rich, she would be all right.

Nigel was helping Peggy to dust the shelves in the shop.

'So what do you plan to do with your ill-gotten gains?' she asked sarcastically. 'You will be less in need of a job than ever.'

'You think I don't work,' retorted Nigel, 'but has it ever occurred to you to consider how much better this shop is doing now that I'm in charge of it?'

Peggy was glad that Nigel saw himself as being in charge of the shop. She certainly hadn't noticed that he had anything to do with it.

Well he had, and the turnover was increasing every week. Furthermore, Nigel had been thinking lately and he was beginning to have a lot of ideas.

By the time Jack came home from a happy four days staying with Daphne Brown, Peggy was fed up with them all. Her mother was dead and nobody seemed to care about her at all, neither her husband, nor her son, nor her daughter who was always with the Willoughbys. Here was she buried in a beastly country post-office with everything conspiring to annoy her while life passed her by. She desperately needed someone to turn to and she hadn't even seen Bruce for ten days. Sometimes she felt like just sitting down and having a good cry.

Jack, on the other hand, was full of the joys of Spring. He had really enjoyed staying in St Albans and now he looked forward to Josephine's summer holidays and to making a layout of the battle of Marengo.

109

Chapter XII

Josephine was delighted to be working for the Willoughbys again, although she knew that the cataloguing was nearly finished and that soon she would no longer have an excuse to go to their house. She had worked for them on and off throughout the Easter holidays but to her chagrin had seen no sign of Julian, who was away ski-ing and then with friends in Scotland. She knew him to have been at home for a week or so but Mrs Willoughby had not asked her to come up during that time.

The cataloguing of the books was, in Mrs Willoughby's opinion, a thoroughly worthwhile job. A number of old and interesting books which nobody knew were in the house had turned up – some first editions and some fine bindings – not to mention various rare Victorian children's books. Admittedly the job had taken a long time because of Josephine being away at school, but Josephine was helpful and efficient and Mrs Willoughby was pleased with her. She quite liked the child and felt rather sorry for her living with that dreadful mother and that old father. It couldn't be much fun.

Sometimes it annoyed Mrs Willoughby to think how her own children were spoiled. They'd always had everything on a plate. She couldn't imagine Julian, for instance, cataloguing one book, let alone ten thousand. She sometimes wondered if he knew which way up to hold a book. Judging from his academic achievements he could neither read nor write. Poor Julian, she did miss him so – she supposed he'd be all right in the end.

It would be a shame when the books were finished with. It was fun doing them and in a way Mrs Willoughby would miss Josephine. They were both rather lonely people, she thought, with little in common, but they both enjoyed the job which created a sort of bond between them so that when one or other turned up an exciting new find, they rejoiced together. Perhaps she would be able to think of something else for Josephine to do. She wondered what.

Josephine was standing on the library steps putting away some books which Mrs Willoughby was handing up to her from the floor.

'I'll be sorry when we've finished,' said Mrs Willoughby. 'It's really been rather fun. I hope you've enjoyed it too.'

'Oh, yes, I've loved it,' said Josephine, sincerely enthusiastic. Despite her disappointment over Julian, Josephine had enjoyed the job for its own sake. Mrs Willoughby was very nice to her and she had had some good meals, some glasses of sherry and had been treated like a grown-up. Colonel Willoughby still called her Joanna but she'd got used to that now and even thought it quite funny, She had been paid generously and had been glad to get away from the shop. There was nothing worse than being stuck with Peggy or Nigel all day although she still enjoyed talking to her father in the garage.

There was only one problem. Josephine blushed whenever she thought of it. She should never have taken those books. There were only three, but still it was wrong and she should never have done it. The Willoughbys had plenty of books and they wouldn't miss them. Even if they did they could easily afford to replace them. They were obviously very wealthy. But what embarrassed Josephine was the fact that she liked Mrs Willoughby. If Mrs Willoughby ever found out, Josephine would die of shame.

She originally planned to take books regularly and sell them in the second-hand bookshop in Exeter, but she had got cold feet about selling them and then, as she grew to like Mrs Willoughby more and more, it became increasingly difficult to steal from her. The three she took, she took a long time ago and now they were a source of deep embarrassment to her. She didn't know what to do with them. She daren't bring them back – in any case she couldn't bring back the one in which she had written – and she was terrified of someone at home finding them.

There was no doubt that *Tess* had aroused a certain interest when she had first shown it around at school, but after one girl

111

said, 'I bet you wrote in that yourself,' she put it away, mortified, and never brought it out again. At the moment the three books were wrapped in brown paper and hidden under a loose floorboard in her bedroom.

Josephine did not have the same qualms about the money she took from the till. She loathed her mother and considered that Peggy treated her badly. So she could see no reason why she shouldn't look after herself. It wasn't even stealing.

'I think we've done enough for today. Shall we have a cup of tea?' said Mrs Willoughby as Josephine climbed down from the steps and rubbed her hands together to remove the dust.

Josephine liked the Willoughbys' kitchen when she first saw it but now she had come to love it as much as any room she had ever seen. It was huge, with a stone flagged floor and a large old-fashioned Aga which permanently seemed to need stoking and which took up nearly the whole of one wall. From the dresser hung china cups and jugs of every shape and size. The plates and saucers propped up behind them were hidden from view by bills, packets of seeds and a collection of postcards which seemed to come from all the corners of the earth. A bunch of dried flowers, a string of garlic and a riding-crop also hung from the dresser.

Along one wall was a battered chintz-covered sofa usually occupied by Mrs Willoughby's dog. In the middle of the scrubbed table there was always a bowl of fresh fruit which made Josephine's mouth water. Peggy never supplied fresh fruit on the grounds that it was extravagant and rotted too quickly. Occasionally Josephine had a chance to help herself to some from the shop. The kitchen walls were hung with a few sepia-tinted family photographs including one of a bride whom Mrs Willoughby said was her grandmother-in-law.

Every time Josephine came to the Manor she was given tea or lunch in the kitchen and she had grown to feel completely at home in it. It was certainly much cosier than Peggy's small, neat, modern kitchen which had originally delighted Josephine.

Mrs Willoughby pointed to a tin on the dresser.

'If you look in there,' she said, 'I think you'll find a cake.'

Josephine put the tin on the table and she and Mrs

Willoughby sat down to their tea.

'I wonder where Julian is,' said Mrs Willoughby.

Josephine's heart missed a beat. She hadn't realised that Julian was at home.

'He's not usually far away from the cake. Have some more yourself,' she pushed it towards Josephine.

'When would you like me to come again?' Josephine asked.

'Well, I should think that if you come a couple of times next week we will finish,' said Mrs Willoughby. 'You know I couldn't possibly have done it all alone. I'm very grateful to you and, by the way, I've got something for you. I might as well give it to you now, before I forget – '

She was interrupted by the arrival of Julian.

Josephine hadn't seen him for six months, during which time he had grown taller and even more beautiful.

'Oh, there you are,' said his mother, 'I wondered where you were. Have some cake. And, er, you know Josephine, don't you?'

Julian glanced expressionlessly at Josephine who blushed and grunted hello. He cut a huge slice of cake which he appeared to swallow in one mouthful, took a tumbler from a cupboard and made for the fridge.

Out of the corner of her eye Josephine watched him fill the tumbler with milk. He threw back his head, tossing his thick, golden hair out of his eyes as he did so and poured the milk down his throat. Josephine was deeply moved by the tilt of the head, the shining hair, the thin, elegant neck, the faint protuberance of the Adam's apple and the relaxed attitude of the slender figure.

Mrs Willoughby was not totally unaware of the sexual current which electrified the room as a result of her son's entrance. She looked at Josephine. Poor plain Josephine, she would have to aim a little lower.

'Come and sit down with us and have some tea,' she said to Julian.

Julian half-turned and caught Josephine's eye as she gazed in admiration at him. She blushed again and looked away. Julian shifted his weight from one foot to the other and clenched his cheek muscles.

'No thanks,' he said, 'I've had enough tea.'

Josephine dared to look at him again and as she did so he gave her a long, cold stare.

How she hated him then. The loathsome, conceited creep.

He left the room without another word.

'Well,' said Mrs Willoughby, embarrassed by the tension in the air, 'I expect there's something he has to do. Now, if you've finished your tea, come with me. As I was saying, I've got something for you.'

Josephine gulped down her tea and stood up. She followed Mrs Willoughby through the house to the front hall where Mrs Willoughby picked a book up from the table.

'I thought you might like this,' she said, 'as a souvenir of all your hard work in the library. It may be a first edition, I'm not sure.' She handed Josephine a copy of *Alice in Wonderland*.

'Oh how wonderful!' Josephine was thrilled. A real present from the library. She glanced at the title page: 1867. She would have to find out when *Alice in Wonderland* was first published. But how nice of Mrs Willoughby to think of giving it to her. She was genuinely touched. This she could show proudly to her father. Her mother wouldn't be interested. She thought with horror of the little brown parcel under the floorboard in her bedroom and wished more fervently than ever that it did not exist.

'I'll see you next week, then,' said Mrs Willoughby. 'Tuesday afternoon, if that suits you.'

'Oh yes, thank you,' said Josephine as warmly as she knew how. 'And thank you so much for the book.'

Mrs Willoughby thought that Josephine looked almost pretty with her face glowing with pleasure.

The next morning Nigel went off to the cash-and-carry, to Josephine's relief. She waited for her mother to be busy in the shop and for her father to have disappeared to the garage, then she hurried upstairs and looked around for Mrs Chedzoy. Mrs Chedzoy was in the bathroom cleaning the bath. That would take her a minute or two. Josephine slipped into her bedroom and pulled back the rug to reveal the loose floorboard. In no time she had retrieved the offending parcel, wrapped her jersey around it and sped down the stairs, through the shop and

114

out into the village street.

She heard Peggy shouting as she passed:

'Josephine, what's all the hurry about? Where are you off to like that just when I need you . . . and what's that you've got with you? Josephine . . . .'

But she was gone.

Josephine hurried up the village street until she reached the church, then she cut through the churchyard and climbed over the churchyard wall where she knew there were footholds, out into the fields behind. She looked around her and when she was sure that she could not be seen, she flopped down onto the grass with a sigh of relief. She carefully unwrapped her bundle. *Tess of the D'Urbervilles*, Tennyson's *In Memoriam* and a remarkably pretty little volume of Lamartine's poetry which she had taken for the sake of its binding. Then from her pocket she brought out two firelighters and a box of matches. As she lit the first firelighter her hand was trembling, for she felt she was about to do a dreadful thing. She hated to destroy the books, particularly the Lamartine. The leather was in such good condition still and the book was over a hundred years old. If only she had never taken it, it would be sitting peacefully in the library shelves at the Manor – she decided to burn it first and to get the worst over with. The last to go was *Tess*.

She thought of horrible Julian as she watched the pages curling and blackening in the flames. How she hated him now. How dared he treat her so? She would teach him one day. She wondered how and then she began to see a way. She imagined herself as a famous barrister throwing Julian into confusion by her brilliant cross-examination of him as he stood trial for murder. Then she imagined herself as a consultant in Harley Street – that would be even better. She would be sitting behind a large desk with a stethoscope hanging round her neck and dressed in a white coat.

'I'm very sorry, Mr Willoughby,' she would say, 'but there is absolutely nothing to be done for you. The best you can hope for is another two weeks.' That would wipe the cold, superior look off his face.

Josephine felt liberated when at last the books were burned. She was poking the ashes with a stick, checking that no

115

unburned page remained, when she heard a voice call her name. She turned round in confusion to see the vicar looking over the church wall.

'Well, well, well Josephine,' he said. 'It's you. I smelt smoke and thought I'd better see what was going on. You can't be too careful in this dry weather. Having a little bonfire, were you?'

Josephine had no idea what to say. She stood awkwardly shifting her balance from one foot to the other and glancing down, out of the corner of her eye, to see if any tell-tale print could be seen in the little charred heap at her feet.

'When I was a kiddie,' the vicar went on, 'we used to think of a bonfire as a great treat. We were supposed to be able to light them with a flint in those days. Sometimes we pretended we had, although we always cheated and used matches. Not very honest you might say, but then boys will be boys!' He gave a hearty great laugh.

Josephine thought the vicar looked ridiculous, standing there on the other side of the wall talking about boys being boys. It was a high wall and he was a small man so he must have been standing on tip-toe in order for his chin to be visible over the wall. She could see his hands holding tight to the wall on either side of his ears, and as he laughed his spectacles slipped down his curiously large, fleshy nose.

'I was just going to brew myself a mug of tea, I'm waiting for the water to boil.' Josephine had to think of something to say.

'No harm in that at all, I should say,' said the vicar and disappeared behind the wall with strange suddenness. Josephine gave a sigh of relief and turned her attention back to her charred remains.

Funny child that, thought the vicar as he strolled back across the churchyard. A bit of a loner, I wouldn't wonder. Perhaps he should call round at the post office some time and see if he could interest her in the simple services for everyone which were being introduced in the parish. It occurred to him that she was rather old to be sitting alone in a field making a cup of tea. Perhaps there was more to it than met the eye. Well, as long as it was a meaningful relationship, who was he to say nay. Waiting for the water to boil. Heavens above! And he began to sing.

Josephine was somewhat surprised when she heard his rich, mellifluous baritone echoing back across the wall:

'And he sang as he watched and waited till his billy boiled,
You'll come a-waltzing Matilda with me?
Waltzing Matilda, Waltzing Matilda . . . .'

The singing finally faded away and she thought the time had come to go home. The funny thing was, she was sure that the vicar had believed she was waiting for water to boil. Couldn't he see that she had nothing to boil it in? What a silly old fool he was.

'Waltzing Matilda, waltzing Matilda, you'll come a-waltzing Matilda with me,' Josephine sang as she came back into the shop.

'Well,' said her mother, 'you sound very pleased with yourself. It's not often we hear you singing. But instead of singing so much, you might think of me for a change and give a hand in the shop . . . and, I ask myself . . . what have you been up to all morning? If you've been chasing after boys, my girl, there'll be trouble. You've no time for that sort of thing – and let me warn you, Josephine, that the boys in this village are not your class – well, except for the Willoughby boys and I don't suppose you would be their type . . . .'

Josephine sighed, walked out through the back of the shop and slammed the door. She decided to go and see her father in the garage. At least he would be pleasant to her.

Later, as Jack filled a jug of water to put on the table for lunch he sang quietly to himself, 'Waltzing Matilda, waltzing Matilda . . . .'

'I can't imagine what you lot have got to be so happy about today,' snapped Peggy. 'That silly song's beginning to get on my nerves.'

That afternoon Nigel was left in charge of the shop while Peggy went to Exeter. She just had to have her hair done.

Nigel asked Josephine to give him a hand to move a few shelves.

'Do it yourself, you lazy thing,' said Josephine sourly. 'I'm not here to wait on you.'

117

Nigel sometimes felt so intensely irritated with Josephine that he was frightened that one day he might strike her. The silly child seemed to put herself above everyone else and as far as he could see it hadn't done her any good spending all that time with the Willoughbys either. It just made her even more pleased with herself. She was always going on about what the Willoughbys had for lunch, what the Willoughbys' kitchen looked like and what the Willoughbys' dog did, until you were fed up to the back teeth with the bloody Willoughbys. Last night she'd been boasting about some book Mrs Willoughby had given her. Couldn't shut up about it. She must have shown it to her father about ten times during the course of the evening. She never mentioned that Willoughby boy though, and in Nigel's opinion it was the boy that really interested Josephine – not the dog or the books or Mrs Willoughby. Nigel had seen that boy around the village a couple of times. A supercilious little beggar. Well Josephine would soon learn, no boy like that would give her a second look.

Sometimes Josephine reminded Nigel of Suzanne. Neither of them very attractive girls – but Suzanne was definitely the nicer of the two. It was a shame to compare her to Josephine. Poor Suzanne. He occasionally felt sorry for the way he had walked out on her. After all, like everyone else, she probably needed someone. She had been clinging all right, and that was what had driven him away in the end, but from time to time he realised that he even missed the clinging. No one here ever looked pleased to see him come in or sorry to see him go out.

Jack was nice enough, but Jack was a gentleman and Nigel had the impression that underneath he was probably indifferent to his stepson's presence in Chadcombe.

Running a village shop wasn't the most exciting thing in the world but it was a pleasant enough way of life – or would be without Peggy and Josephine under the same roof. He could imagine that with someone like Suzanne it might even be quite enjoyable. He imagined Suzanne, in her tight jeans, her bottom a bit too fat, arranging the jams on a shelf, carefully wiping the shelf before she did so. And he saw himself coming back from the cash-and-carry. Suzanne's face would light up and she would hurry out to help him unload the car. Perhaps

118

she would cook nice meals like her mother. After supper they would watch television and never quarrel about which channel to choose. Then of course there was the problem of bed. He still didn't relish the thought of Suzanne in bed. But perhaps if he could come to terms with that he would be able to overcome his other problem.

A wry smile crossed his face as the thought of coming across Suzanne in a lonely street. That would soon stop her clinging.

Josephine came into the shop.

'Haven't you finished with those shelves yet?' she said.

Nigel gave her a rather peculiar leer. You too, he thought. And he chuckled to himself.

'I'm glad you're so cheerful,' said Josephine.

'I was wondering what you wanted in here. Me to get out of the way, I suppose, so that you can put your hand in the till.'

So Nigel did suspect her. Josephine was not wholly surprised. She knew him to be sneaky and prying. She looked him straight in the face.

'If you tell anyone,' she said, 'you will regret it. Do you remember years ago, when you first came to stay and the police came to call? You lied to them about the day you went to Exeter. Of course I don't know what you were doing, but I know you lied to those policemen.' She tossed her head, rather, she thought, as the detestable Julian might do, and walked calmly out of the shop, leaving Nigel to his own devices. She was very pleased with herself. She had been saving that precious piece of information for a long time now.

Chapter XIII

Jack was seventy-two, the winter had seemed to be a long one, and now that spring had eventually come he was feeling rather under the weather. It annoyed him to think that many men of his age still dug their gardens or rode to hounds. The President of the United States was more or less the same age and only last week Jack had listened to an octogenerian cyclist on Radio 4, recounting his experiences of bicycling across England by the Fosse Way. Jack had no desire to rule the United States, nor indeed to bicycle along the Fosse Way, but it did distress him to feel so permanently tired, besides which his hip was giving him a certain amount of trouble. He had lived a reasonably healthy life and he was not a self-indulgent man although of course he liked his occasional pint. He had always looked forward to living to a healthy old age and he was beginning to wonder whether things were going to work out that way.

Perhaps a change would do him good. He even thought of asking if Peggy would like to go away with him for a week-end. He wondered if she would agree to come. They could go down to Torquay and stay in a nice, comfortable hotel. Or a few days in Hove or Brighton might be pleasant. They could walk along the sea front and Peggy would surely enjoy being waited on in a comfortable hotel.

Easter wasn't until the second half of April that year, which meant that Josephine was not due back from school for a couple more weeks, and Nigel, who had now been with them for over a year, could easily look after the shop. As far as Jack could see, Nigel was entirely responsible for the shop these days anyway. He had even been trained to run the post office.

During the fifteen months or so that Nigel had been with them the shop had changed entirely. Jack was amazed when he first saw Nigel making dainty displays of avocado pears and peppers on the counter. After avocados came anchovies and olives and home-cooked ham. Now they even had Italian salami and German bread. The latest delicacy to tempt the villagers was taramosalata. It was a long time since Chadcombe had seen plastic wrapped squares of processed cheese. Instead a large cheddar stood on the counter and disappeared each week with incredible speed. Now Nigel was planning to introduce brie. He was on excellent terms with the cheese man and spent hours talking to him and tasting cheeses each week when he came round.

To begin with, Jack had been certain that Nigel was making a mistake and Peggy snorted in disdain as more and more exotic foods appeared. Never mind foods – now they even stocked French cigarettes for the sake of a lecturer in French from the university, who lived in the next village. The lecturer in French came for his Gauloises and, being a greedy man, he bought avocados and salami as well. His wife was so impressed with the shop that she bought nearly all her groceries there. She was confined to her house with small children and found it easier than going to Exeter. It was a little more expensive, she realised that, but she reckoned to save money on petrol. And she was not the only one.

The turnover of the shop had increased dramatically, as all the local gentry now had accounts there, and to Jack's amazement, Nigel proved fairly successful in persuading the villagers to try new things.

What Nigel always said was that you had to be prepared to provide a service. He didn't mind letting people have things after hours – he would even deliver to people's houses of an evening. What you lost on the swings you gained on the roundabouts and the proof of the pudding was in the eating. Jack was delighted with the results when he came to do the accounts – a job which he now did in combination with Nigel.

After her initial irritation, Peggy could not fail to be rather pleased by what had happened. For one thing, her bank account was in a slightly healthier state and for another the shop had become a livelier place. She congratulated herself on having had the good sense to sell so many new and interesting things.

Jack saw no point in saying that Nigel and not Peggy should be congratulated. A quarrel was the last thing they needed. He felt that he and Nigel and Peggy had been living at particularly close quarters for the last few months, partly because Jack had found it too cold in the garage, despite his gas heater, to spend much time there. Throughout the winter the cold had seemed to penetrate his bones – perhaps this was something to do with old age – and so he had stayed in the house or the shop for most of the time. It had all been rather claustrophobic really and this was another reason why he felt that he would like to go away.

It was a pleasantly mild morning, so when Jack had finished reading the *Telegraph* he decided to go into the garden with a pair of secateurs. He had been intending to prune his few roses for some days now and he felt he should take advantage of the finer weather. The first daffodils were beginning to open and Jack spent an agreeable morning pottering around the garden.

When lunch-time came he was glad of the opportunity to sit down. Peggy had laid the table for two. She was busy opening a tin of ravioli when Jack came into the kitchen.

'Where's Nigel?' he asked.

Nigel had gone off for lunch at the pub with the cheese distributor.

'Let me do that,' Jack suggested, taking the tin-opener with which Peggy was struggling. 'You might have found it easier if you had put down your cigarette.'

Peggy had a cigarette in her mouth and her eyes were screwed up against the smoke.

'Could you keep an eye on the shop if Nigel isn't back in time?' Peggy asked. 'I've had enough of this place. I'm going in to see June this afternoon. We thought we'd do a bit of shopping. Cheer ourselves up.'

Jack pushed his lukewarm ravioli unenthusiastically around his plate. He thought he was hungry when he was in the garden, but suddenly he had no appetite.

'I think we both need cheering up,' he said. 'In fact I was wondering if you would like to come away with me for a few days. I thought we might go to Torquay – or Brighton – and stay in a really nice hotel – on the sea front. Perhaps it's not really your idea of fun, but it would be a break and it would give me great pleasure if you would come.

Peggy was flabbergasted.

'Good heavens above!' she said. 'What will you think of next?'

Fancy Jack wanting to take her away after all these years. If he only wanted a break he could always go and see that Daphne Brown. She felt quite tempted. The idea of a posh hotel was not to be laughed at.

'Oh yes, I'll go,' she said and felt a fleeting twinge of guilt as she saw Jack's face relax. Perhaps she was occasionally a little hard on the old boy. He got on her nerves but then so did Bruce these days – not to mention Nigel. All men were the same really. Little boys at heart and thoroughly selfish.

'Let me make us some coffee,' said Jack, standing up.

'Don't you fancy your ravioli then, dear?' Peggy leaned forward and asked in a voice filled with new-found compassion.

Good lord! thought Jack. She didn't sound like herself at all. Really rather more like Mrs Thatcher. He smiled to himself.

'Ah well,' he said as he put two cups of Nescafé on the table and sat down again, 'perhaps the sea air will bring back my appetite, and with the warmer weather I'll be able to spend more time in the garage.' Besides deploying his men, he enjoyed poring over maps of military campaigns and there was really no room for them in the sitting room.

'Where would you like to go?' he asked.

'Brighton,' Peggy was adamant. Brighton was where she would like to go.

When Nigel came back from lunching with the cheese distributor, just before Peggy left for Exeter, he was amazed to find his mother and stepfather in such a cheerful, almost childish frame of mind. There was a rare lack of tension in both their voices, and Jack was smiling gaily as he washed the dishes.

'What's up with you two?' he asked.

'We're off to Brighton,' Peggy announced, snatching up her bag and making for the door. 'Darby and Joan are off to Brighton – but I must fly now, or June will be waiting.'

You could have knocked Nigel down with a feather.

When Peggy had gone, Jack went into the sitting room and

123

turned on the television. He told Nigel that he had been in the garden all morning and was feeling a bit tired. There was no doubt about it, he couldn't do as much as he used to do. In any case he wanted to watch the third episode of *Crown Court*. He must know if that man was going to be found guilty.

Nigel thought he might watch *Crown Court* too. It was quite an intriguing programme, but just as he was about to sit down he heard the shop door and he disappeared to attend to the customers. Within ten minutes Jack was asleep in his chair.

Peggy and June met for a coffee in Exeter and over their coffee they planned their afternoon's shopping. Peggy would be needing some smart clothes for Brighton.

June was amazed by Peggy's sudden decision to go away with Jack but Peggy thought it might teach Bruce a lesson. She'd had enough of his high-falutin ideas about the Caribbean and Spain and so forth. They never came to anything. It was all just talk. She couldn't see why she shouldn't go away with her own husband. Bruce would soon see – Jack might not be very exciting, but then he was old now – and let there be no mistake, Jack had been very good-looking as a younger man and he was a real gentleman. It might not be the Caribbean but if Jack said they were going to Brighton, you could be sure they would go. Peggy could do with a few days in a nice hotel and Jack had assured her it would be a nice hotel – one of the classier ones on the sea front, she was sure. And who was Bruce to dictate where Peggy should go with Jack?

A week later Peggy set off with Jack for the Grand Hotel in Brighton. It would cost a bit but after all, as Jack said, they didn't go away often so they might as well do it in style.

Peggy was delighted. She bought herself a black tailored costume for the occasion and some bright red high-heeled shoes with a bag to match. She wore red gloves and a little red hat too.

Nigel was to drive his mother and stepfather to the station since Jack had decided that it would be much too tiring for him to drive all the way to Brighton, and anyway it would be much more agreeable to go by train. Besides he, as a senior citizen, could travel on British Rail for next to nothing.

Jack was ready to leave long before Peggy, looking meticulously neat with shiny shoes and his regimental tie. When Peggy eventually appeared in all her finery Nigel nearly laughed.

'Good Lord,' he said, 'anybody would think you were going on your honeymoon.'

'You look very nice, dear,' said Jack. 'Now come along or we will miss the train.

The Grand Hotel was splendid. It quite came up to Peggy's expectations and she realised that it made her feel, for once, as if she really did belong to the upper crust. Jack had reserved a room with a sea view and as the porter took them up in the lift she felt he must be admiring her elegance. And as for Jack, well, he ought to be proud to be seen with such an attractive, younger woman.

And of course he was. As they sat in one of the lounges beneath a grandiose ceiling, sipping sherry before dinner, he put out his hand to take Peggy's.

'Thank you for coming with me,' he said. 'It's very sweet of you. Don't think that I don't understand that it must some-times have been dull for you with an old husband like me, but we have had some good times. Do you remember the cruise? Now I shall never forget that cruise.'

Peggy really felt quite moved. She dabbed her eyes daintily with the corner of a lacy handkerchief. Poor old Jack. What a sentimental old fool he was at heart.

'I always say,' she said, 'that life's what you make of it.'

Quite frankly Jack had never heard her say so before and neither had her behaviour ever led him to suppose that such was her philosophy. But still they were enjoying themselves and this was no time to be argumentative.

Perhaps tomorrow Jack would be able to persuade Peggy to visit the Royal Pavilion, although she was really more interes-ted in the idea of going to the Dolphinarium. She had been told that there the dolphins sang and danced like real people and were very friendly. Apparently they were the most intelligent of all animals and could not only add up and subtract but could do the most complicated long division. Dolphins were known to be able to speak several languages, to decipher codes and to tell the time.

125

As it happened Jack thoroughly enjoyed the dolphins. They were enchanting creatures. Peggy enjoyed them too – you couldn't help loving them – but she was sorry not to have heard them speak. In fact she thought the whole thing was rather a cheat. After all, when you paid all that money you at least expected to hear them say something.

But Peggy had no complaints about the hotel. It was nice to see such high standards these days. She and Jack enjoyed eating a leisurely breakfast in their bedroom. And the view of the sea was lovely. There was no comparing it to the Caribbean, but Jack had done his best and for once she did not feel like complaining. The Caribbean was one thing and you had to face it, Brighton was another. Both very nice in their different ways.

After breakfast on the second day Peggy rang for room service. She wanted some laundry done.

Jack observed that the hotel offered no service which Peggy was prepared to overlook. He only wished that she would learn to adopt a slightly less haughty tone when speaking to the staff. Perhaps it was something to do with women. Didn't they say that it was the British wives who had lost India? Well he wasn't really too sure about that. After all he had been in India and knew something about it. A long time ago now, of course. In fact he knew perfectly well that Peggy's tone had nothing to do with women in general as he couldn't imagine someone like Daphne Brown – or Bobby for that matter – speaking to people in the same way. He supposed sadly that it was too late for Peggy to change now.

When Peggy had dispatched her things to be washed, she and Jack set out for a walk along the Esplanade towards the Palace Pier. There was nothing Peggy used to enjoy so much, years ago, as slot machines but they had changed completely since she was young. It seemed to be all Space Invaders now. But she would still like to try her hand at them. Just for a laugh.

Jack thought the Fun Palace would be too crowded and noisy. It was certainly not for the likes of him. If Peggy wanted to go there he would happily wait outside for her. There were seats along the front and Jack could sit on one of them and look at the sea. It was a pleasant, sunny day although a little cold.

'I'll be waiting here,' said Jack as he sat down. 'Don't waste all your money.' He was glad to be wearing his British warm as the wind off the sea was quite penetrating. The sea itself was choppy and Jack settled down with pleasure to watch the breakers crashing on the pebbles and to listen to the cry of the seagulls, the thud of the waves and the drag of the shingle. How lovely it all was. Jack had always liked the sea and could not imagine why anybody should prefer the Mediterranean to the wilder Northern seas. What was that about a dirty British coaster? Something through the channel in the mad March days? It was March now . . . . He wrapped his coat more tightly around him.

Peggy was gone for about half an hour. She came back just in time to see Jack collapse. As she walked towards him he seemed to lurch forward suddenly before landing in a crumpled heap on the ground. She screamed and broke into a run. She reached him and knelt down beside him.

'Jack, are you all right?'

Jack moved slightly and gave a sort of groan.

Peggy was not the sort of a woman to deal with an emergency but soon a small group of people had gathered around the scene and someone had run to telephone for an ambulance. Although it seemed to Peggy like an age, it was only a matter of minutes before Jack had regained consciousness and had been helped back to the seat. He was dazed and seemed to have some difficulty in speaking.

At the hospital the doctor told Peggy that Jack had suffered a mild cerebral embolism of the kind often described as a spasm. He would be quite fit in a day or two but the incident should be regarded as a warning. Certain risk factors would require treatment.

'Don't upset yourself so, Mrs Bennett,' the doctor added. 'Your husband is in good hands and will be perfectly all right so long as he takes care.'

Peggy couldn't stop crying. The whole thing was so unfair. She and Jack hadn't been away together for years and then this had to happen. She couldn't afford to go on staying in the Grand Hotel while Jack was in hospital, and what was she supposed to do, alone all day, in a strange town? Nobody seemed to think about her. It was all right for Jack, he had the entire National Health Service breathing down his neck.

She thought she would go home alone and send Nigel up with the car to fetch Jack. That would be the best thing.

In fact Jack was discharged two days later and Peggy stayed on in the Grand Hotel. They had been planning to stay there for four nights anyway. She divided her time between the hospital and the hotel. In the hotel she made long and expensive telephone calls to Nigel, Bruce and June, or sat in the bar talking to whoever was prepared to listen to her woes. Such a nice business man from Birmingham bought her a drink one evening and, as he was alone himself, invited her to join him for dinner. It was nice to know that despite all her troubles she was still an attractive woman.

Jack was mortified to think that he had spoiled the trip. Of course it was not really his fault and, for that matter, it could have been a great deal worse. Thank God it had only been a mild stroke! Everyone was more than kind and the hospital staff were wonderful. But poor Peggy. It must have been dreadful for her. She must have been terrified when she found him lying on the ground. And such a pity when they had been having such a pleasant time that this had to happen. He wondered how Peggy was managing on her own. She was not someone who knew very well how to deal with solitude.

When Jack and Peggy finally reached home Jack was feeling pretty ropey. The long train journey had really been a bit too much for him and he thought he ought to go straight to bed as he had been told to take things easily. He began to climb the stairs.

'I'm sure you feel tired,' snarled Peggy, 'but what about me, struggling across England with the luggage and an invalid in tow? I should think that if anyone needs to lie down, it's me.'

Jack winced at the sound of her voice. That dreadful selfishness could never be laid for long. Why, he wondered, were women so selfish? Some women anyway. As he stepped into his pyjamas it occurred to him that selfishness was the most ridiculous form of self-protection since people isolated themselves by it. He wondered how unhappy Peggy really was, and if she was even seriously aware of her own unhappiness – as opposed to her discontent. He himself was not unhappy, not really happy either – except when he had good news from Josephine, or when she came and sat with him in the garage. But he was contented. Yes, on the whole, he was a contented man.

As he lay in bed he began to think about the sea and travel and all the places he had visited during his lifetime, and then he drifted off to sleep.

Peggy did not feel at all herself. The whole thing had been a bitter disappointment. Would Nigel get her a drink? A drop of brandy would do. And where was her lighter? She must have left it on the train. Get me some matches, will you? Jack was lucky that she'd been there to run back and forwards to the hospital which was miles from the hotel. Fancy having a fit like that when you were on holiday.

'Poor Jack,' said Nigel.

'Poor Jack? Jack's all right. As right as rain if you ask me.'

In fact Jack was diminished by his stroke. He never felt the same again, and most people remarked that he seemed to have aged overnight. He moved more slowly, occasionally slurred his speech, walked with a stoop and had great difficulty in gripping with his left hand.

Chapter XIV

Nigel was never a particularly talkative fellow but it seemed to Jack that recently he had grown increasingly morose. Perhaps he was bored with life at Chadcombe despite his enthusiasm for running the shop. It wasn't a very exciting life for a young fellow when you came to think about it, and he must be getting on for forty now.

In fact Nigel was thirty-five and in some ways happier than he had been for years. He had a few friends or at least acquaintances in the neighbourhood with whom he went out to the pub and that, he always supposed, was all a man needed, but all the same something was wrong. He felt frustrated by the fact that the shop was not really his and he was worried about what would happen if Jack died. He could not imagine what Peggy would do but hardly supposed that she would be prepared to stay on in Chadcombe. Not that he could possibly think where else she would go. She didn't seem to be seeing so much of that fellow of hers lately although she still spent a good deal of time gadding about Exeter. She had relinquished nearly all work in the shop and had even had the good grace to tell him the other day that she had no idea what she would do without him.

At other times he was aware of her intense hostility. Peggy was glad that Nigel and Jack seemed to get on so well, but she couldn't help thinking that an old man was an odd companion for someone of Nigel's age. Then came the jibes about marriage and girlfriends.

Perhaps, Peggy had suggested recently, with one hand on her hip as she flapped the other in the air, he was one of 'those'. Well, you never knew, did you. She had read somewhere that every time you travelled on a bus there were three of 'those' – she performed the same ridiculous gesture – travelling with you.

Nigel was furious. His mother was an intensely irritating, utterly selfish, stupid woman. She wasn't even a good mother. Look at the way she ignored poor Josephine. Not that he could really blame her for that. But still, Jack managed to be good to the child.

Sometimes Nigel wondered about his own father who had left them when Nigel was nearly sixteen, but of whom he had strangely few, remarkably indistinct memories. He was left with the impression of a good-looking, moustachioed character with thick hair and a loud voice. He remembered boasting at school about his father's Jaguar with its white-walled tyres, but he also remembered feeling that because of his inadequacy on the sports field, he was a disappointment to his father. Once when Nigel had watched him through the open bathroom door, naked to the waist, scrubbing his armpits, he had felt a violent wave half of envy, half of disgust at the broad shoulders and muscular, hairy chest. His own pale, thin chest had barely expanded since.

One day the Jaguar with its white-walled tyres had sped away from the house in Aldershot, never to be seen again. After that Nigel received a couple of Christmas cards from his father and, on one occasion, a postcard from Lima. There was nothing more. Now he didn't even know if his father was still alive.

Well, Nigel was certainly not one of 'those', and neither was he remotely like his father although he had begun to fear that he shared his father's attitude to Peggy, so that sometimes he wished he were in Lima himself. But he had been abroad during his short time in the Navy and had hated what he had seen.

Early in life Nigel had learned that no good came from depending on others for comforts, and yet now he was in an agony of indecision. Should he, or should he not contact Suzanne? He could ask her down to stay at Chadcombe and he felt sure that he would be glad to see her, but if she came, Peggy would begin to ask questions, even Jack might raise an enquiring eye-brow and God only knew what conclusions Suzanne would leap to. Nigel had not heard from Suzanne for well over a year now, during which time his behaviour had

131

been impeccable (the guilty urge had almost died away completely, he felt), but it never occurred to him that she would not be waiting patiently to hear from him.

The other alternative was for him to go to London and see her there. That would be far more convenient in many ways but he felt that perhaps he might not be welcome at her parents' home. He supposed that he could just go to the shop and see her there – but then he might not find her. She might have changed jobs or she might even be away for the day.

Eventually, after weeks of indecision, he decided to write. There could be no harm in that and if Suzanne refused to see him – which was of course out of the question – the humiliation would be private and therefore minimal.

Dear Suzanne (he wrote), How are you? I hope you are keeping well and that your parents are keeping well too. Since I came to Devon I have taken over the management and supervision of my mother's shop with all that that entails. I have introduced a variety of new items which were hitherto considered unsuitable for the market in these parts. Resulting from the initiative which I have taken, the returns from the business are commencing to show an appreciable improvement or, as you might put it, things are looking up! I am planning a trip to London during the last week of this month and would consider meeting you for lunch if that would suit. I await your reply at your earliest convenience.

Yours sincerely,
Nigel

Once he had posted the letter, Nigel began to feel quite nervous and to doubt the wisdom of his action, while at the same time looking forward to the next development.

He was, in fact, quite right in supposing that Suzanne's life had remained much the same for the last two years. She still lived with her parents and she still worked in the same department store – still in the same department. She was nearly thirty now and although she supposed that she might never marry she had not given up hope on the very deepest

132

level.

Her mother, for one, wanted to know where she was ever going to find a husband if she didn't make an effort and go out and look for one. She knew that her mother was right really and she was determined to do something about it. So far she had written to the problem page of a woman's magazine from which she received the inevitable reply, advising her to go to evening classes where she would find people who shared her interests. She then made the fatal mistake of going to flower arrangement classes where there were thirty women and only one man who was obviously not on the look-out for a wife. After the flower arrangement classes, she tried needlework classes with the same result. Of course that had been a silly idea but she could hardly affect an interest in metalwork. Her mother said she was being silly and that she must be able to find something between metalwork and flower-arranging. What about photography? Suzanne had no camera and besides, what little confidence she'd had was now shattered, so she stayed at home waiting for a miracle and eating chocolates.

A minor miracle happened in the shape of a letter from Nigel. When Nigel first left London, Suzanne fondly imagined that, away from her, he would realise the force of the passion which had been burning within him and that he would return to London, throw himself at her feet and declare his undying love before whisking her away to a life of pastoral bliss in the Devon countryside. Occasionally it crossed her mind that he might be homosexual. But for some reason she felt sure that this was not the case. She waited a little while and then, in desperation, wrote him a friendly note, just to keep him in touch with the gossip. She wrote a couple more times, but he never answered and so she was finally forced to put him out of her mind.

'You have a letter this morning, dear,' Mrs Evans remarked one Monday morning as she handed the envelope to her daughter. 'It has a Devon post-mark. Now I wonder who that can be from. Who would you be knowing in Devon?'

Suzanne took the letter. Her heart missed a beat. It was Nigel – after two years he was coming to whisk her away. She hardly dared to open the letter.

'I hope it's not from that useless Nigel. You wouldn't be wanting to have anything to do with him, I shouldn't think. Not after the way he treated you. Sit down and have your breakfast then – and take your time over your letter.' Mrs Evans poured out a cup of tea for Suzanne.

'Leave the girl alone, Lily, for God's sake,' said Mr Evans, looking up from the *Daily Express*. 'She'll tell you in good time if there's anything you need to know.'

Suzanne glanced at her watch.

'Look Mum, I must fly,' she said, 'or I'll be late for work. I'm sorry I haven't time for the tea. See you this evening – bye, Dad.' She grabbed her coat and bag and, clasping her unopened letter in her hand, she made a dash for the door before her mother could say any more.

Nigel's letter was hardly expressed in terms that could give Suzanne much hope. She read it over and over again on the underground and she read it again at work. Where was the burning passion, the undying love for which she so yearned? But still he had written – after two years he still thought about her. She consoled herself with the knowledge that, at the best of times, Nigel was not a demonstrative person which meant nothing for she knew that calm exteriors often hid turbulent natures. Still waters run deep and all that.

During her lunch hour Suzanne wrote back to Nigel saying that she would be pleased to see him and suggesting that he came to the shop at lunch-time on the Wednesday of the week he would be in London. She posted the letter on the way home.

In fact Nigel had no intention of staying a week in London, but he did not want Suzanne to think that he was going there just to see her. He would take a day return and catch an early train from Exeter.

On the Tuesday evening before the meeting Suzanne washed her hair and put it in curlers. In the morning she put on her best dress and, instead of her anorak, her nice new winter coat.

'Well we are smart this morning,' Mrs Evans commented as her daughter left for work. 'Are you going anywhere special?'

It was only just gone twelve when Nigel arrived in the West

134

End. He was feeling nervous and beginning to wish that he had never come. Thinking that a drink might calm him down, or give him courage, he went into a pub where he whiled away half an hour before making his way to the shop and the record department where he immediately noticed Suzanne handing a parcel to a customer. She turned round and as she saw him appear from behind a display of vocals her whole face lit up. She came towards him wreathed in smiles.

Nigel felt strangely touched. He couldn't remember ever having been smiled at quite so spontaneously or warmly.

They had lunch in the same pub where Nigel had been earlier. Gammon steaks, chips and peas and a glass of beer each. The conversation flowed with surprising ease. Nigel talked about Chadcombe and Jack and Peggy. Suzanne had never heard him so forthcoming. She talked about the people at work, and her needlework classes and her father who was due to retire next year.

Curiously relaxed, they strolled back towards the shop. Suzanne was late for work, but, uncharacteristically, didn't worry. Nigel even took her arm. As they reached the shop she turned to say goodbye.

'It's been lovely seeing you again, Nigel, and thanks for the lunch. I hope . . . .'

'Will you marry me?' Nigel suddenly blurted out. 'That's why I came to London – to ask you.'

Suzanne was stunned – quite stunned. For a moment she thought she was going to faint and she gripped Nigel's arm to steady herself.

As for Nigel, he couldn't believe that he had heard right. O Christ! O Christ! He hadn't got a house. He hadn't got a proper job and he had never wanted a wife.

'Yes Nigel, I will,' whispered Suzanne. Her voice had almost entirely deserted her. 'But I'm late for work. I must go now,' she stammered. 'When shall we see each other?'

Nigel could think of nothing but escape.

'I have to go back to Devon this afternoon. I'll be in touch,' and then with a sudden surge of pity for plain, hopeful Suzanne with her tiny shining eyes, he leaned forward, kissed her on the cheek and was gone.

Well, that certainly called for another drink – and a cigarette. He didn't smoke very often. Peggy's smoking habits were enough to put anyone off. He arrived back at the pub just in time for last orders and bought a packet of cigarettes and a double whisky.

In the pub and all the way home in the train Nigel went over and over what had happened. He had never intended to ask Suzanne to marry him. Of that he was sure. He had spoken on impulse – without thinking. It was almost the same sort of impulse that used to drive him to do those other silly things. And, in another way, it was as if he had said what he did out of politeness. There had been some kind of need to say something – but not that – oh no, not that.

By the time the train reached Taunton, Nigel had had a few drinks in the bar and he was beginning to feel more in control of the situation. Life with Suzanne would, after all, be infinitely preferable to life with Peggy. What, when you came to think about it, was so ridiculous about the idea of marriage? Other people had been married before and some of them even seemed to be quite happy. He must not allow himself to see all women in terms of Peggy. Then he thought of bed – bed – bed – bed – he wished he could stop thinking about it. If it came to the crunch he supposed he could manage – it wasn't as if he were impotent. Suzanne was not very beautiful of course, but then he was no Adonis himself. Nigel had no illusions. But she was nice and kind and had been touchingly pleased to see him.

At Exeter Nigel left the train feeling slightly drunk. He had parked Peggy's car at the station to save her the trouble of meeting him, but he didn't want to go straight home. Instead he would go for a little walk, sober up a bit before he went back to Chadcombe. As he walked his mood changed – as it had many times that day. He saw marriage as a total loss of not only his independence but his personality. He saw himself as a Tom Thumb with a giant Suzanne bending over him, picking him up and putting him down like an object, tidying him away into a drawer, drowning his tiny voice with loudly spoken opinions. It was unbearable. Peggy he imagined siding with Suzanne. He could hear her strident tones saying that he had always been a disappointment, a disappointment to his mother, a

136

disappointment to his father and a disappointment to the Navy.

He quickened his pace and strode determinedly towards the darker back streets . . . .

Nigel did not reach Chadcombe until after midnight. He was glad to find when he came in that both Peggy and Jack had gone to bed. He did not feel like talking to anybody. He had walked for a long time before his fatal encounter with the two policewomen in plain clothes. At the police station he was treated to stern disapproval by the women and to sneering innuendo by the men. He made his statement as clearly and calmly as he could before leaving to drive home. He was surprised that they allowed him to drive, since it must have been clear to them that he had had too much drink. Perhaps the effects had worn off, but he fully expected to spend a night in the cells. He was given bail on his own recognisance and told to appear in court on Monday.

The next morning he awoke to realise the full horror of the preceding day and swore never to leave Chadcombe again. There at least he was at peace.

As far as he could see, there was only one thing to be done and he spent most of the morning doing it. He wrote a long, convoluted, grovelling, pompous letter to Suzanne in which he explained that she had misjudged him. He was not the person she had taken him for, and he felt that he could not marry her under false pretences. He was a lonely man with personal problems which he would not normally dream of discussing, but unfortunately he had been apprehended in Exeter on his return from London and was shortly to face a charge of indecent exposure. He could offer no explanation except that he was in an emotional state and had had too much to drink on the train. He called himself a rat, an inhuman bungler and a thoroughly unsatisfactory person unfit to mix with nice girls like Suzanne. He begged her forgiveness and hoped that she would soon forget him and find someone more worthy of her.

When Nigel had finished writing he felt utterly exhausted. He had never confided so openly to anyone in his life before. He addressed the letter and posted it with a first-class stamp before he could have any second thoughts – although he could always snatch it from the postman who came to empty the box.

137

But he didn't.

Peggy was calling him from the shop. He'd been away all yesterday and now he was wasting time writing letters. Would he please come and help? People were queueing for their pensions.

Suzanne spent a desperate two days after her lunch with Nigel. Two days which seemed like an eternity of silence beset by doubts. Had he had second thoughts? Why didn't he telephone? She dared not announce to the world that she was engaged. The whole thing seemed too ridiculous. Where was the fiancé? Where was the ring? When was she getting married? Where would she live?

On Saturday morning she received Nigel's letter. Relief swept through her at the sight of his handwriting, and then when she read the letter all was explained. Poor, poor Nigel. Now he would really need her to stand by him.

Nigel spent the weekend worrying about his pending case and the scandal it would cause in the neighbourhood, so that he was no longer thinking about Suzanne. He had written to her and considered that she and everything to do with her were best forgotten, so he was taken completely by surprise when he returned from the magistrates' court on Monday to find that a letter had come from her in the afternoon post.

Nigel was heartily relieved that the case was over. It was a first offence, he was known to be a person of good character and, as he explained to the magistrate, he had been under some emotional stress on Friday and had had a drink or two on the train. He was not used to behaving in this way and could assure the court that there would be no recurrence of the incident. He added that he was thinking of getting married in the near future. The magistrates took him at his word, fined him £50 and let him go. But he was still worried by that little paragraph which was bound to appear in the local paper. The news would be round the village in a flash – unfortunate choice of word – Peggy and Jack would find out in no time and life at Chadcombe would be intolerable.

He went into the kitchen where he turned on the kettle for a cup of tea. Suzanne's letter was lying on the table. He hesitated before opening it. What more could Suzanne have to say to

138

him?

She had to say that of course she would forgive him and stand by him and that nothing would prevent her from marrying him if that was still what he wanted.

What a tenacious, clinging person she was! Yet the letter expressed genuine sympathy and understanding and not a hint of shock. And Nigel could not forget how pleased she had been to see him.

At supper-time that evening Jack was busy talking about the Conservative Party Conference which was taking place at Blackpool that year. He had been watching it on the television during the afternoon.

Peggy was more interested in what Nigel had been doing – sidling off to Exeter so secretively – dressed in a suit too.

Nigel thought it quite unnecessary for him to have to account for his every move. He would not dream of asking Peggy where she was going but he supposed that the time had now come when he ought to tell them that he was getting married. That bombshell was intended to deflect their attention from the other bombshell which would surely follow soon.

Certainly Jack forgot the Conservative Party Conference and Peggy stopped worrying about where Nigel had been that day.

Nigel was a dark horse! There was no doubt about that. But where was he going to live? How could he afford to support a wife? And how did he think that Peggy could manage the shop without him now that his stepfather was a semi-invalid?

There were endless matters to be discussed and Peggy had every intention of dealing with them all in turn.

Suddenly Nigel felt a surge of excitement. It seemed to him that his mother had never, ever before shown so much interest in him.

Chapter XV

Everything was turned upside down by Nigel's marriage which took place in the spring of the following year, a week after Suzanne's thirtieth birthday. For one thing the post office was hardly big enough to house so many people. Jack, who was growing increasingly immobile, had ever more difficulty in making his way to the garage at the back of the garden. He was frustrated by his inability to get there and missed the quiet reflective times he spent with his soldiers. He consoled himself with reading but then his eyes were not what they were and he tired easily. The television was some consolation, but the main trouble was that the house was too crowded. Everyone was on top of you.

Nigel too felt the overcrowding acutely. He had almost called the whole thing off again when he saw the van arriving from Exeter with the double bed. The men had scraped the paint on the stairs as they carried it up to his room into which it barely fitted. Peggy had been standing on the landing with a cigarette in her hand, directing the proceedings. Mrs Chedzoy had stopped hoovering to come and have a look and a giggle.

Suzanne was delighted by everything. It was such a change after Cricklewood. Her mother had warned her of the dangers of living with her in-laws. She knew that her mother was right and thought that a job – which she would need anyway – would get her out of the house and ease the situation. She applied for and was given a job in Marks and Spencer in Exeter. It meant an early start to catch the bus in the morning but she enjoyed the job and was quite invigorated by the change in her circumstances. She supposed that eventually, somehow, she and Nigel might have a place of their own.

Nigel's main concern was to stay in the shop at all costs. Jack could not go on for much longer and he was determined to take

140

over when the time came. He was still not sure what he would do about Peggy. Financially he should be all right. He had long since ceased to be a lodger at the post office and now took a share of the profits. Besides, he had the little bit of money left to him by his grandmother, and Suzanne's salary was a help.

On the whole he did not regret having married. In some way he felt that a wife gave him more standing and established him as a serious member of society, and anyway Suzanne was good-natured and enjoyed cooking. The standard of meals had risen sharply with her arrival. Perhaps Suzanne's greatest quality was her ability to endure Peggy's ill-temper without ever complaining or answering back. Sometimes Nigel felt swamped by her careful mothering and on these occasions he usually vented his spleen on Peggy.

Nigel had another reason for wishing to stay in the shop. In the shop there was no room for children. Children. A wife was one thing, but children had not even crossed Nigel's mind until Suzanne began to talk about them. Oh, no thank you, they weren't having any children.

When Suzanne first went to work at Marks and Spencer Peggy was delighted. She imagined an endless supply of new outfits, all of which would be available at half-price. But she was soon to discover that Suzanne was quite a little prig and not prepared to play the game. Fancy a prig like that marrying Nigel after what he had done. Mrs Chedzoy had quite rightly commented on what she had read in the paper. If she hadn't, Peggy would have been the last to know. The shock and humiliation at the time had been dreadful. Her son! In a way she was glad to know that he still had one. She had begun to think that it had dropped off long ago. Luckily the engagement had happened at about the same time to take people's minds off the disgrace of the other thing. Not that Peggy would ever forget a thing like that. Not Peggy. Oh no. She was utterly disgusted and would never be able to see Nigel in the same light again. Jack was different – he had taken the whole thing quite calmly and then refused to discuss the matter.

It was three months now since the wedding, which had taken place quietly in a registry office in London with a nice lunch afterwards at Suzanne's home. Considering the class of people

141

the Evanses were they had done it all very nicely and Peggy was pleasantly surprised. Now it was summer and Josephine was due home after her last term at school. She was due to go up to Manchester University to read history in the autumn. Both Peggy and Jack were extremely proud of that.

Jack was, as usual, looking forward to Josephine's return. The house would be more crowded than ever, but that would not matter with Josephine around. Jack had felt for his daughter throughout the term. She had worked so hard for her 'A'-levels and he prayed that she would be rewarded by excellent results. He was ambitious for his daughter and was sure that if she continued to work she would go far. He was sorry not to be able to drive up and fetch her from school, but he had not really been up to driving since his stroke. Certainly it would be out of the question for him to go so far.

The last three years at school were a long hard slog for Josephine. She worked partly because there was nothing else to do and partly because she wanted to go to university and get right away from home. She didn't know what she wanted to do after university. Go into industry perhaps. Anything that would help her to escape from the stifling atmosphere of Chadcombe. School, of course, was not much better since she had never managed to make any close friends there. Perhaps it had become slightly less bad as her fellow pupils grew accustomed to her over the years and their merciless teasing lost some of its spite and turned to almost affectionate mockery. But she didn't think that there was anybody there whom she would really mind never seeing again.

She looked forward to going to university where she expected to find serious-minded, hard-working girls like herself. Perhaps she would even find a boyfriend. Not someone like Julian Willoughby – she loathed the memory of him – but a sensible boy with whom she could discuss her work and the state of the world. A marriage of true minds. She sometimes asked herself if such a thing were ever really possible. Her father and mother were hardly a case in point, but she often wondered what her father's first wife had been like. When she was younger and alone at home one day, snooping around the house and looking in drawers, she had come across a photograph of the first Mrs Bennett. She looked rather pretty. But Josephine had never dared to ask her father about her.

Peggy collected Josephine at the station. It was a nuisance about Jack not being able to drive any longer.

'You'll find things quite changed at home,' said Peggy. 'Nobody else is allowed in the kitchen now Madam has taken over. I sometimes think I'm hardly the mistress of my own house.'

Much as she hated Chadcombe, Josephine was looking forward to coming home so as to see her father. She felt sorry for him now that he had aged so much and grateful to him for all the letters he had written to her throughout the term. He was the only person who bothered about her when she was away or who had ever encouraged her over her work. When the exams came round other girls received endless pictures of pussy cats with good-luck messages on the back. She could do without any pictures of pussy cats but she did feel that her mother might have sent some message.

Jack was really cheered up by Josephine's return. She had grown into such a nice girl, always ready to go for a walk with him, or to help him up the garden to the garage. With her for a companion he might manage to start on a layout of the battle of Waterloo. He couldn't really imagine why he had never done one before. Together they discussed every aspect of the battle and the reasons for Napoleon's defeat, which were not always so simple as they were sometimes supposed to be. They discussed Josephine's future and her reading programme for the summer. She had been sent an enormous reading list by the university.

Sometimes in the past Jack had found Josephine rather moody, but this holiday she seemed to have changed. Perhaps she was delighted to have finished with school or perhaps she had just grown up a bit. He noticed that she even managed to keep a civil tongue in her head when speaking to Peggy and Nigel.

Jack had long since learned to accept Peggy as she was. At times like when they had gone to Brighton or now, when she sat with him and watched a television film, he could be glad of

143

her company. She could even be quite funny occasionally. But he would never be able to understand her total indifference to her children. Josephine he adored, so she at least had one parent – an old and decrepit one – but a parent. Poor old Nigel had never had anyone. Of course he was grown up now and had Suzanne. Suzanne was all right in her way. Would never have been Jack's cup of tea though. Jack quite liked Nigel. The boy had made something of the shop. But Jack flattered himself that he had had a bit more spirit in his day than Nigel could muster in a lifetime.

A funny thing, old age. Well, funny wasn't really the word. When you were young you never imagined it could happen to you and then, suddenly, one day, there you were, unable to see, unable to hear, unable to drive a car, unable to sleep at night and with less and less to do in your waking hours. Jack felt he was prematurely old. He wasn't yet seventy-five. He often thought of poor old Maurice Brown. Maurice had seemed so old to Jack only a few years ago and now Maurice was dead and Jack was not far behind. No good could come of dwelling on the matter and Jack was glad that he could still take an interest in reading and in day-to-day affairs. There was no point at all in giving up – it could only make you more miserable.

When Josephine's 'A'-level results came in late August Jack held his breath as he watched her open the envelope. He dared not look at her face. Without a word she handed him the piece of paper.

'A, A, A,' he read. He had lived a long time, but moments of such acute joy and pride were rare.

He took his handkerchief from his breast pocket and blew his nose.

'Well done,' he said.

He cried again when Josephine left for Manchester. He must be getting a bit senile, what with all this blubbing. The worst of it was that he would have liked to drive her up there. But of course he couldn't and there was no use expecting Peggy to do it.

'Drive her to Manchester!' Peggy thought he must be daft. What was wrong with British Rail? Josephine had grown up now and the sooner she learned to stand on her own feet the better.

Jack missed Josephine dreadfully when she had gone. It was silly really, since he was used to her being away at school, but her letters home seemed sad and frightened. Manchester was such a huge, dark city and she was having difficulty in finding her feet.

University was not at all as Josephine had imagined it would be. She found that her fellow students lacked her intense interest in their work. They spent most of their time making a loud noise in pubs. Some of the girls seemed no less silly than those with whom she had spent so many years at school. The work was difficult and, try as she might, she was not achieving the standard of academic brilliance of which she had dreamed. Neither was anyone else, with the difference that they didn't seem to try as hard as she. She was relieved when the first term drew to a close and it was time to return to Chadcombe. Chadcombe of all places. She wondered if anything in life could ever fulfil its promise.

Christmas was quite different that year. It was the first Christmas since Nigel was married and Suzanne brought a new enthusiasm to the occasion.

Josephine had not taken a liking to Suzanne. She regarded her as a dull intruder who must be quite peculiar if she were prepared to marry Nigel. But she had to admit that the Christmas pudding and the turkey were an improvement on the usual Chadcombe post office fare of chicken and peas followed by Walls chocolate ice-cream. She was embarrassed by the generosity of Suzanne's present, and somewhat amazed by the magnificence of the Christmas tree and the proliferation of holly and paper chains. It was as though Suzanne, in the face of all evidence to the contrary, was the only one prepared to pretend that they were an ordinary, happy family – whatever that might be.

Whenever she could, Josephine escaped to the garage where she helped her father plan the battle of Waterloo. He had not managed to do very much on his own while she was at university. Although she enjoyed being with her father and was pleased to be away from the others, she was sometimes irritated by what appeared to her to be Jack's complacency.

145

There must be more to life, after all, than sitting in a garage with a lot of toy soldiers. She had loved those soldiers as a small child and then she had gone through a period in which she despised them. Now she just liked them in a detached sort of way, and was glad that they made her father happy.

At times Jack referred to Napoleon as 'I'. Like the time when he said: 'I never really believed that Blücher could recover from Ligny in time to join Wellington at Waterloo.'

'Daddy,' said Josephine sternly, 'did you say "I"?'

Jack's eyes twinkled.

'Don't worry my dear. I'm not mad. It's just a little fantasy I sometimes indulge in. Where would we all be without a little fantasy?' Where indeed?

One day Julian Willoughby came into the shop for some cigarettes. His exquisite teen-age beauty had faded as his features had coarsened slightly and he had put on weight. This did not prevent him from being accompanied by a long-legged, giggling blonde.

Josephine was in the shop at the time and was horrified to see him arrive. She had not seen him for a long time although she knew from his mother that he had joined the Army on leaving school. Far more embarrassing than Julian was the long-legged blonde who blushed and simpered and who recognised Josephine from school. Josephine had hated her at school and she hated her now. She hated all those people. Perhaps she hated too many people. But she didn't care. One day, somewhere, she would find the kind of people with whom she could really communicate. She just wondered where they were.

'Are you helping or are you just going to stand there getting in everyone's way?' Nigel asked as he pushed rudely past her.

'Oh shut up,' she said and marched out of the shop.

Peggy was sitting in the kitchen painting her nails and half-reading a novel by Barbara Cartland.

'I would have thought you might have grown out of that rubbish by your age,' sneered Josephine.

'There's no need to be so superior, dear,' said Peggy. 'It's only a little bit of fantasy. Fantasy never did anyone any harm.'

Josephine walked out of the kitchen then and slammed the

146

door. What on earth was the matter with them all? Simpletons. The whole lot of them. Sometimes she longed for the good old days when she used to help herself from the till. But Nigel had put a stop to all that long ago and now she had to find other ways of taking her revenge on Peggy. She didn't really have a hold on Nigel any longer. She wondered if what he had been up to all those years ago when he lied to the police was the same thing for which he was caught last year. It probably was, but she wasn't interested any more. He made her sick. He must have a warped mind or something.

She was fed up with everybody and was beginning to look forward to going back to Manchester.

In her second term she began to be happier and even made friends with two of the girls who lived in the same hall of residence as she did. The three of them took it in turns to take coffee in each other's rooms. They talked about their work, about the iniquity of government cuts in education, they complained about their lecturers, about the other students and about the cost of books and they even discussed the possibility of sharing a flat in the second year.

By the summer term Josephine had met Russell. Russell was a ginger-haired geography student in the same year as Josephine. He came from Watford where his father had a small double glazing firm. His father was hoping that when he had finished his degree he would join the firm. But Russell, who was an only child, had other ideas. He wanted to be a teacher but his father was all against that. There was no money in teaching and if Russell didn't join the family firm he would be looking a gift horse in the mouth. You couldn't pick and choose what you did in these days of unemployment. Not even if you had a degree in geography.

Josephine began to think that she too might go into teaching, but she was in no hurry to make up her mind.

Both she and Russell were depressed at the thought of returning to their families for the long summer holiday. Josephine couldn't face the over-crowding, the bickering and the boredom with only her father and the soldiers for solace, and Russell longed to escape from an over-protective mother and a dominating father, so they agreed that somehow they would find the money to hitch-hike round Europe. Josephine was contributing towards the cost of her own university education with the money her grandmother had left her, but she thought she would just be able to manage the holiday. Russell wasn't sure what he would do. Borrow from the bank, he supposed. Banks were very helpful towards students these days.

Just before the end of term Josephine and her two girl friends found a flat for the following year. The only disadvantage was that they would have to pay for it throughout the holidays but Josephine didn't really mind when she discovered that if they stayed there during the holidays they would be entitled to a rent rebate from the council. Besides, she would not have to go home. She would stay in Manchester until she went abroad.

Josephine, her two girl friends and Russell all moved into the flat in the last week of term. Josephine was beside herself with delight although she felt a faint twinge of pity for her father whom she knew must have been looking forward to her return. She would have liked him to come up and see her in Manchester – she had explained awkwardly to her friends that her father was old enough to be her grandfather – but she knew that he would never come. He really did have a problem getting about these days and there was no hope of persuading Peggy to drive him. Not that Josephine would have wanted to see Peggy.

As far as Peggy was concerned Josephine was welcome to stay in dirty old Manchester. If she preferred a nasty little student flat to a proper home and a nice family environment then that was her look-out. Josephine needn't think she would be missed at home. Oh no. If her room was free – who knows – perhaps Suzanne would think of having a baby.

Peggy was not interested in babies – especially not in grandchildren – and it was no good Suzanne thinking that if she had a baby she could dump it on Peggy whenever she felt inclined. All the same Peggy was forever squinting at Suzanne's stomach. Of course Suzanne was quite a fat girl so it might not be easy to tell if she were pregnant. Josephine was the one she ought to be worrying about. She was the one who would be pregnant – traipsing around Europe for half the summer alone with a boy.

When Jack learned that Josephine would not be coming home in the holidays he was bitterly disappointed. It was selfish of him, of course, to be so upset because in fact he should have been glad that she had settled down so happily at university and made friends. Perhaps she would come home for a weekend. He rather wished that he could meet her friends, but then she had never brought any school friends home either. He felt a surge of bitterness towards Peggy. It was she who kept them away.

Josephine did come home, but only for a few days at the end of August after she came back from abroad.

She had gained in confidence, but her new-found confidence made her assertive and, Jack felt sadly, rather know-all. She seemed to have left them all behind without any regrets. Her fleeting visit was soon over. When she left she promised to write often but Jack only received two brief notes from her between then and Christmas which she decided to spend with Russell's family that year.

Chapter XVI

Time had gone by so quickly – particularly the last two years since Josephine had gone to Manchester – and now Peggy's sixtieth birthday loomed horribly near. She tried not to think about it. When she did she was frightened. Sometimes she was even frightened by the sight of her reflection caught in a shop window as she passed. Not that she looked sixty. Not at all. No one would ever guess her age. Most people would probably put her at somewhere in her late forties. That at least was a comfort.

As for Jack, he had turned into a really old man. Anybody would think he was ninety the way he shuffled about the place these days. Peggy wondered how much longer the old boy had to live. If he had another stroke, then that would probably be it. Of course he didn't have much left to live for now. He kept on about Josephine and her academic success. He had just heard that she had passed her second-year exams brilliantly and of course that had set him up. It was almost as though he had been the one taking the exams. And then there was that silly battle of Waterloo which had him so worked up. He'd never finished it, but it was hardly Peggy's fault if he couldn't get to the garage without help. He should never have put those soldiers out there in that garage. The steps which led up the garden were quite hazardous enough for an able-bodied person – let alone a shaky old man with a stick.

It was all right for Josephine. She liked the soldiers, so it was no trouble for her to take her father to see them whenever she came home, but then she hardly ever came home nowadays. And then there was Nigel. He sometimes took Jack to the garage but the trouble was that once he got there he could never get away again. You couldn't leave Jack in the garage because he couldn't get back without help.

Sometimes Jack talked about moving the soldiers down to the house, but that was out of the question. Where on earth could he put them?

Peggy was seriously worried about what would happen to her when she was widowed. She didn't really fancy the idea of staying on in the shop with Nigel and Suzanne. Of course she could always sell it, but where would she go? She'd thought a great deal about the problem.

There was always Bruce, but Peggy was never quite sure how much she could rely on him when it came to the crunch. After all, he'd promised to take her to the Caribbean one day and she hadn't noticed going there yet. She was unlucky really. There was no getting away from that. Throughout her life she had had to do with people who let her down. Time and time again. Take Bruce. He was another one who was only out for what he could get. Supposing Jack lived for another three or four years – Peggy would be well into her sixties by then and Bruce might think that it was too late for them to start again. Besides Jack was only seventy-five and he could live for another fifteen, or even twenty years. Poor devil. No, she wouldn't wish that on him – not the way he was going. You had to hope for a merciful release.

Peggy began to think more and more about the possibility of leaving Jack before it was too late. It would just be a question of persuading Bruce. She had been seeing Bruce for six years now and they'd had their ups and downs – like anybody else. A couple of years back Bruce's wife had found out about Peggy and had made a terrible scene. A lot of business she had to make a scene after the way she'd been carrying on for years. The truth of the matter was that her fellow had given her the push and she had just wanted to take it out on someone else. Anyway, Peggy and Bruce hadn't seen each other for a while after that. They'd remained friends of course. Then, when Bruce's wife started to play up again, Peggy and Bruce got back together.

Now they usually saw each other once or twice every ten days, and they usualy had a good old laugh. You had to laugh. They no longer made any secret of their friendship. Where was the point? Jack never asked where Peggy was going. It didn't seem to bother him.

The only trouble with leaving Jack was what to do with the post office. Peggy would really want to sell it. For one thing she would need the money. But if she sold it – what would she do with Jack? So long as Nigel and Suzanne were running the shop, she could rely on them to look after Jack until he died. Then of course she would sell up. But if she didn't sell the shop at once Bruce might say that they couldn't afford to go away together. Bruce was forever going on about money – mortgages and tax and this and that. She sometimes thought he must dream of money. It was terribly unfair of Peggy's mother to have left her money to Nigel and Josephine. What did they want with money? That little bit of money would have come in handy.

If Peggy stayed on in the post office herself she dreaded to think what would become of her. She would go crazy. There were no two ways about it. She had stuck Chadcombe for ten years now. Ten of the best years of her life had been wasted in that village. Quite simply wasted. The time had really come to think about herself for once. If Peggy had a fault it was that she was too good. She'd allowed everyone else to walk over her for long enough. She no longer dreamed of a hotel in Spain, partly because she felt sure that she would never be able to persuade Bruce to live out of England. He wasn't likely to want to live in Alicante, now was he? Not if he didn't even want to go to the Caribbean for a fortnight. A nice little flat in town would be ideal. She would happily settle for that.

One evening at about half past seven, just as Suzanne was clearing away the supper, the telephone rang. Suzanne answered it.

'Mrs Bennett, it's for you,' she said and scowled disapprovingly at her mother-in-law.

It was Bruce. His wife was away and he was feeling pretty down what with one thing and another. Why didn't Peggy jump in the car and come for a drink?

Peggy was delighted. She dashed upstairs to change her clothes and to touch up her make-up. Suzanne sat down in front of the television and picked up her knitting – socks for Nigel who had disappeared into the shop to clean out the deep freeze. She sighed and glanced at Jack who was filling his pipe, apparently unaware of anything else. Poor old thing, she thought. That woman leads him some dance.

Suzanne's smouldering dislike of Peggy seemed to grow more intense daily. What a wife. What a mother. Suzanne even blamed Peggy for the fact that she and Nigel didn't have a baby. Peggy was in the way and Peggy made Nigel nervous. Suzanne longed for a baby but at the very mention of babies Nigel flew off the handle. He said that there was no room in the post office and that anyway they couldn't afford a family. Suzanne was becoming increasingly desperate and was not at all sure how to cope with the situation. Her sex-life was not quite everything that she had hoped it might be. Nigel was all right really – just not very keen. She had to be careful not to upset him or there would never be any chance of a baby at all. She sighed again.

Peggy's painted face appeared round the door.

'Bye bye you two. I won't be back late, but you needn't bother to wait up,' she said and vanished.

Suzanne heard her tripping away on her high-heeled shoes and a moment later the front door slammed.

Good riddance, thought Suzanne. And don't worry, no one had any intention of waiting up. She looked at Jack again. He hadn't said a word but was impassively watching the television.

'Would you like me to make you a cup of coffee?' she asked him.

'Thank you, my dear. That would be very nice. This strike's very worrying,' he added, turning back to the television. 'I wonder how long they will hold out.' He drew on his pipe.

Peggy drove quite fast and reached Bruce's house just after half past eight. It was a fine, late June evening. As he opened the door Bruce said:

'Lovely evening. Let's get out of town. Hop in my car and we'll go to the Smugglers' Arms. Haven't been there for ages. If I put my foot on it we'll be there by nine.'

As they drove through the lanes Peggy wondered what exactly she was going to say to Bruce. She was glad they were going to the Smugglers' Arms. It had a nice atmosphere and they usually had a good time when they went there, although she remembered the last time she had tried to persuade Bruce

153

to run away with her. That was when she had wanted them to go to Spain. They had been in the Smugglers' Arms then. Well that hadn't worked out at all. Never mind – she wouldn't mention abroad this time. All the same she decided to tread carefully. Wait until they'd had a few drinks.

The Smugglers' Arms was crowded and Bruce had trouble parking his car. People were sitting out in the garden and there was a carefree, holiday atmosphere.

Peggy asked for her usual Bacardi and lime and Bruce had a double Scotch. They took their drinks outside.

'You know that ad for Bacardi?' said Peggy.

'Which ad?' Bruce asked.

'You know, the one where Telly Savalas drinks Bacardi . . . .'

Bruce grunted.

'Well, would you believe it, he really drinks it – even when he's not advertising it. It says so on the ad.'

'Can't stand the stuff myself,' said Bruce. 'Give me Scotch any day. Well, how's things at Chadcombe? Suzanne pregnant yet?'

Peggy snorted.

'Suzanne pregnant. She'd be lucky. I don't think Nigel's up to it – I don't know what's the matter with the boy to be honest.'

Bruce laughed. It always amused him to talk about Nigel whom he considered a right nutter.

They were on their third round of drinks when Peggy decided that the time had come for her to ask how life was going for Bruce at home.

Judy, his wife, was making a nuisance of herself. Peggy might have guessed as much. Judy was usually making a nuisance of herself. She was ever so neurotic and she made life a misery for poor Bruce.

'She just never lets up,' said Bruce. 'She seems to think I'm made of money. Last year I gave her a new hair-dryer, a food-mixer, a microwave oven, an electric carving knife,' he counted the gadgets off on his fat fingers as he spoke. 'This year she's had a video and a new sewing-machine and it's not yet July. Now she wants a three-piece suite. I can't afford the HP on that lot. Anyway I can't see what's wrong with the three-piece suite

154

we've got. To be quite frank with you, I'm fond of that three-piece suite. Had it for years.'

Peggy was tremendously sorry for Bruce. No man could be expected to put up with that sort of behaviour.

'To be perfectly honest,' said Bruce, 'I reckon we were all better off when she had that bloke of hers. Ugly bloke. Looked like a bit of a nancy boy to me. But he couldn't stand the pace either, poor fellow. She was bleeding the little bugger white. You should have seen what she got out of him. Perfume, jewellery, lighters . . . .' Bruce started to count on his fingers again: 'underwear, chocolates, house plants . . . .'

Peggy felt a twinge of jealousy.

'I call that disgusting,' she said. 'Quite disgusting!'

'Don't let's worry about her. Have another drink,' said Bruce. 'Same again?'

Peggy would love another, but she thought they ought to go inside. It was getting dark and even a little chilly. Besides there were mosquitoes about.

They moved into the pub. Bruce carried their two empty glasses in his right hand. His left hand rested on Peggy's neck.

'Where's Judy now, then?' Peggy asked as they found a table in a corner and sat down with their new drinks.

'God alone knows,' said Bruce. 'She walked out in a temper about half an hour before I rang you.' He paused. 'Said she was never coming back.'

Peggy felt a thrill of pleasure.

'Oh Bruce dear, you poor soul!'

'Don't worry, said Bruce. 'She's done it before. More times than I can count. She'll be back in the morning.'

Peggy's heart sank. She lit a cigarette. She didn't say anything for the moment. Where, she wondered, should she go from there?

They stayed at the Smugglers' Arms until closing time. When the barman called for last orders, they decided to have just one more for the road.

'Don't you think, love,' Peggy began hesitantly, 'that if Judy keeps saying that she wants to go away for good, then you should let her go? The way I see it is that once something's over – really over – then you should just put it behind you. Let it die

155

a natural death. Where's the sense in dragging on in a marriage that makes you both miserable?'

'Well, we're used to each other,' said Bruce. 'And then we're financially tied to each other.'

'Financially tied! My foot! More like she's ruining you, if what you've just been telling me is true. A man like you needs a good woman – someone unselfish and loving. You deserve better. You know you do.'

'Judy's not all bad. She keeps the house nice so I suppose she thinks she has a right to a few of the good things of life.' Even through the haze of alcohol Bruce was beginning to sense the drift of the conversation.

'I like that!' said Peggy. 'I keep the house nice, but I wouldn't dream of asking Jack for all those things. Mind you, I do think that we need a video. Everyone else has one and they're ever so useful especially if you're going out and there's something on the telly which you don't want to miss.'

'You can come and look at ours if you want,' said Bruce, taking advantage of the digression. 'We might even hire a few saucy films. Make a night of it!' He gave a broad wink and pinched Peggy's knee. He glanced at his watch. It was just on eleven.

'Time, gentlemen, time,' called the barman. The few remaining customers began to stand up and move towards the door.

'Come on love, bottoms up,' said Bruce.

Peggy drained her glass and stood up carefully. On the way out she tripped and nearly fell to the floor. Luckily she just managed to save herself by catching on to the bar.

'Steady there – all right then?' said the barman. 'Mind how you go.'

Bruce winked at the barman.

'It's these silly shoes,' said Peggy. 'They don't make anything properly these days.'

Outside the air smelt of honeysuckle and roses.

'Pity to have to go back into town on a night like this,' said Bruce, sniffing the balmy air.

They climbed into the car and Bruce fumbled in his trouser pockets for the keys, stretching out first one leg and then the other. In the end he had to get out of the car again before he could find them.

He took a minute or two to fit the key into the lock, then, with a burst of acceleration, he backed out of the parking space.

'Lights! You've forgotten your lights, mate!' yelled a man who was standing in the car park as they sped away.

'What's the matter with him?' asked Peggy.

'God knows,' said Bruce. 'Must be barmy. I've seen him before, haven't you? He's always in the Smugglers' Arms. Probably had a few too many.' They roared off up the lane. A car coming towards them flashed its headlights.

'Lunatic, trying to blind me,' said Bruce.

'It's ever so dark tonight,' said Peggy.

'Christ!' said Bruce, 'I haven't got my lights on. No wonder.'

'That's better,' giggled Peggy as he turned them on.

As they drove on Peggy warmed to her theme.

'You know, Bruce,' she said, 'you and I, we're not as young as we used to be. It's no good pretending. And here we are – both of us – trapped in rotten marriages . . . .'

Bruce let out an expletive as he swerved to avoid a hedgehog.

'. . . I know that years ago I wanted us to emigrate to Spain and all that. Of course that was silly. I realise that now. It would have been too much of an undertaking. Altogether too difficult. But you know we shouldn't waste any more time. We mustn't pass up our chances. You say yourself that Judy makes your life a misery . . . .'

'You leave Judy out of this,' snapped Bruce. 'Judy's my problem.'

'That's what I mean. She's a problem. Why don't you just forget all about her? I can leave Jack and we can settle down together.' She snuggled up to Bruce's shoulder.'

'Look here,' he said, 'I know what you're up to and it's time you realised that the answer is no. We've had a nice evening. So let's leave it at that.'

Peggy began to snivel.

'Don't you ever think of me?' she whined. 'How do you think I can stand it – cooped up in that post office all day with Nigel and Suzanne and Jack who's practically senile now. You don't

157

know how he's gone down hill lately.'

'Look, Peggy, Judy and me, we've been together for twenty-five years. Where's the sense in breaking that up now? You can't just forget somebody when you've been with them that long.'

'But you're not happy, you're always telling me that you're not.'

'And what makes you think I'll be any happier with you? You've run through two husbands, who's to say you wouldn't run through a third?'

'Oh, Bruce, that's not fair – Bruce, you're frightening me! Please drive a little slower.'

Bruce hurtled round another bend, roared up behind a motor-bike and began edging out as though to pass.

Peggy gripped the edge of her seat. She knew Bruce fancied his driving and she was used to speeding back with him by night ever since that first time when he'd taken her out to dinner.

'Live dangerously, that's my motto,' said Bruce as he edged out again.

'Not too dangerously,' said Peggy. 'I want to get home in one piece.' The mention of home brought her back again to her subject.

'Oh Bruce, I don't think you know how awful it it living with that lot. Imagine me when Jack dies – all alone with Nigel and Suzanne. Josephine doesn't count any more. She never comes home. I don't know what I've done to deserve such an ungrateful child. That girl has no thought for her mother – none at all. And as for Nigel and Suzanne, they won't want me around when Jack's gone. I'll be all alone with not a friend in the world to speak of – just think of that – after everything I've done for them. But with you, love, it could be different. You and I – well, it's not too late for us to make something of it together. I saw my mother dying all alone and I don't want it to be like that . . . .'

'For Christ's sake, can't you shut up!'

Bruce swerved out again. There was just room to pass the motor-bike and plenty of time; he could see the lights of an approaching car, but it was still a long way off.

'. . . I don't want to be left all by myself when I'm old –
Bruce – can't you see – I'm frightened . . . .'

The motor-bike was forced off the road and disappeared into
the ditch as Bruce sped by. Peggy covered her face with her
hands and screamed . . . . The oncoming driver had no time to
stop and no room to make way. The two cars collided head on
and a sheet of flame burst from the tangled metal.

A few moments later a bruised and shaking motor-cyclist
crept out of the ditch.

'Jesus Christ,' he muttered. 'Did you ever see such a
bleeding pile-up?'

The following morning the unpleasant task of identifying
Peggy's charred remains fell to Nigel. He and Bruce's wife
Judy met at the mortuary. They could find nothing to say to
each other.

Chapter XVII

Josephine felt strangely unmoved by the news of her mother's death. She hated her mother and saw as little of her as possible, but except for when she was very young, she had never wished her dead. Josephine was not likely to miss Peggy, as far as she could see, Peggy's existence had been fairly pointless but all the same she would have expected to feel some kind of emotion on hearing of the death of a parent. Instead she felt nothing. It was almost as if she had read in the newspaper that a famous actor had died. Something to register in a vague sort of way and then to put out of your mind.

Of course she could not put Peggy's death out of her mind because she would have to go home for the funeral and at home she would be confronted by her father's grief which might be painful, and she knew not what else. How, she wondered, was Nigel taking it – and Suzanne? Nigel, she thought, was a nasty, selfish creep. What he felt about his mother she could not imagine. She supposed that he must have disliked her but then he chose to live with her which was odd in itself. As for Suzanne – well Suzanne was a dull, uninteresting person, hardly worth considering, in Josephine's opinion, but then she wasn't really nasty. In fact she wasn't nasty at all. Josephine could imagine Suzanne walking around snivelling, her face all puffed up from crying. Suzanne was the sort of person who cried every time a baby bird dropped out of its nest.

Josephine packed a few things in a small bag and left for the station. Her two girlfriends said goodbye with long faces. They put their arms round her and looked understanding. They agreed behind her back that it was really bad luck her mother dying just now when the exams were over and there were so many parties going on. But of course it would have been worse for poor Jo if she had died during the exams.

Russell accompanied Josephine to the station. He felt a duty to take care of her in her hour of need. He knew that she had not liked her mother, but poor kid, she must feel terrible now, and yet she was being really rather brave. She didn't show her feelings at all.

She leaned out of the window to kiss Russell goodbye as he stood on the platform, and clung to him desperately. Russell supposed that her deep sense of loss occasioned so much passion and returned her embrace with an understanding fervour.

A porter walked along the platform slamming doors as he went and then, with a jolt, the train began to move.

Russell watched Josephine leaning from the window in her turquoise T-shirt and waved until she was carried out of sight. Then he turned and shuffled off in his sneakers and dirty jeans. He was beginning to worry about himself and Josephine. She was cleverer than he and more hard-working; besides, quarrels about money – whose turn it was to buy the bread and so forth – had begun to upset their relationship. He looked at his watch. Half past eleven. He might go back to bed for a bit.

Josephine sat down and took out her book – *These Old Shades* by Georgette Heyer. She had worked so hard for her exams that for relaxation she had taken to reading books which she would formerly have despised. She was lucky, she thought, as she opened the book, to have found Russell. She hoped that one day she would marry him. It was a pity that he didn't work harder, but she had decided that next year she would be able to organise his work for him. If he took her advice he should do quite well in his finals. She was sure that if he worked harder he would have more self-respect and if he had more self-respect he wouldn't feel the need to be so argumentative about shopping and other day-to-day matters.

She began to read, but found that she was unable to concentrate. As her thoughts turned to Chadcombe, she stared out of the window at Greater Manchester slipping by under a hazy summer sky.

She wondered what would happen now that Peggy was dead. Her poor father. He would feel dreadfully lonely. Nigel and Suzanne weren't much company. Neither for that matter

161

was Peggy, but Josephine presumed that despite their differences, there must have been some sort of link between her parents – a shared past or something. Admittedly it was hard to imagine what. It was a shame that Jack had grown so frail. If only he were less dependent on other people, life would look less bleak for him.

It was starting to rain when, five hours later, the train reached Exeter. Josephine felt tired and dirty and apprehensive. Apart from her grandmother's cremation, she had no experience of death and as she drew near home some of the awe of the occasion began to make itself felt.

Nigel was waiting at the station to collect her. Most uncharacteristically he hugged her. In the awkward shiny embrace of his kagoul she began to tremble. Russell and history degrees and Manchester and even her two girlfriends seemed to belong to another world, like scenes and characters from a film or a dream. Only this shiny blue kagoul and reedy, kinky Nigel existed – and Exeter station in the rain – and presently that horrid, claustrophobic shop would come into being and silly fat Suzanne and a poor, sad old man. Somehow there would be a gaping space left empty by a strident, selfish, painted woman. She began to cry and Nigel tightened his hold. She was not crying for Peggy – why should she cry for her? Her tears were for her father and for him alone. She swore to herself that she would come home and see him more often. At least once a month.

In the car Nigel explained the circumstances of Peggy's death to Josephine. He had told her on the telephone that there had been a car crash but had not gone into any further details.

Josephine was disgusted. She had found out years ago that her mother had been seeing another man, but somehow she had assumed that that had long since been over. Peggy would have been sixty soon and to carry on like that at her age was revolting.

'Death must have been instantaneous,' said Nigel. 'At least we know that she didn't suffer, poor thing.' Nigel was haunted by the horrible sight which had greeted him at the mortuary that morning.

'She may not have suffered,' said Josephine brutally, 'but everyone else around her was always made to suffer.'

Nigel was shocked by Josephine's impiety and they drove the rest of the way home in silence.

Suzanne had not gone to work that day and Jack had spent the whole morning and most of the afternoon pottering around behind her, trying to help in the kitchen and offering to make cups of unwanted tea at all hours. He felt useless and ashamed at having had to allow Nigel to go and identify his mother's remains. Nigel had also contacted Josephine and rung the undertaker and the vicar. In fact Nigel had been very helpful. But where did that leave Jack? Jack firmly believed that the balm for all sorrow lay in action, and here he was with nothing to do.

Of course he had expected to be the first one to go. And indeed he should have been considering he was sixteen years older than Peggy, and now there was this bolt from the blue which left him completely stunned. He longed for Josephine's comforting presence.

Jack remembered the pain of Bobby's death. And now he was widowed again. Bobby he had loved and when she died he felt that his heart was broken, that he would never be a whole person again. This time it was different. He did not love Peggy – nor, for that matter, had he ever loved her in any true sense. But in so far as he had chosen to marry her and had lived with her for twenty years – longer than he had lived with Bobby – she had become a part of him.

Peggy's death was appalling, not only because of its terrible suddenness, but because Jack would acutely miss the presence of a very positive existence. She must have been an unhappy woman and Jack felt intensely aware of the part he had played in making her unhappy.

He should have tried to understand her better. Instead he had cut himself off from her and indulged his own interests. He had never tried to include her in any way and he had driven her to seek comfort with that dreadful man. It was entirely his fault. The horrible guilt was almost more difficult to contemplate than the loss he had felt when Bobby died. Of course Bobby had not died suddenly. Jack had been with her through the last stages of cancer. His every waking moment had been devoted to her, either in thought or deed, and he had suffered daily for her. When she died, bereft though he was, he had been glad that she would have no more pain. This was different. There was nothing about Peggy's death which could make anybody glad. Only guilty. Shocked, sad, helpless and guilty.

When Nigel and Josephine reached Chadcombe, Jack was sitting at the kitchen table filling his pipe. In front of him sat a particularly nasty looking cup of cold tea. Suzanne was washing something in the sink. Josephine was shocked by the sight of her father. She had expected him to look unhappy but never had she imagined that a man could look so miserable. His cheeks were grey and his expression was that of someone who has been struck several severe blows across the face. He struggled to his feet to greet Josephine.

'My dear child,' he said, 'how glad I am that you're here,' and he embraced her. 'Your poor dear mother,' he said as he clasped her more tightly to him. 'Poor dear Peggy, I should have looked after her better. I neglected her you know.' He released Josephine and turned to sit down again. 'I neglected her and this had to happen before I realised it.'

'There, there,' said Suzanne, 'don't you take on so. You know it wasn't your fault. Please stop blaming yourself. These things happen and they're out of our control. Josephine, you sit down. You must be tired after your journey. I'll make a fresh pot of tea.' Suzanne's eyes were red from crying and her face looked unusually puffy.

That night Jack couldn't sleep, and the next day he wandered around looking like a zombie. He had difficulty in contemplating the full horror of what had happened. He was consoled by Josephine's presence and at times appalled by his own inadequacy. He felt that he should somehow be arranging things, taking charge, playing a more masterful rôle. It was as though Peggy's death had finally robbed him of all manhood – and now he deserved that punishment. Why, oh why, had he not taken more care of her? He was not such a fool as to forget Peggy's true nature just because she had died, but he could not bring himself to blame her for what she was. He felt instead an overwhelming pity and again and again an image of her sitting

164

in the front seat of a car, terrified in the face of death, her hands raised in horror, flashed into his mind. Poor, poor Peggy. It was not her fault that she had been unhappy – and his thoughts came round again in circles to what he believed to be his own guilt.

He did not really consider the future. Not for several days at least. His mind was occupied by the immediate present and the funeral.

After the funeral – Jack was touched by the number of villagers who turned up – Josephine went back to Manchester, having promised her father to return again soon.

In the days which followed Josephine's departure Jack's remorse grew deeper. But it was not Josephine whom he missed, it was the electricity of Peggy's personality. At times he felt her presence acutely. He awoke at night to hear her voice. 'It's time somebody gave some consideration to me,' he would hear her say. Or, 'Nobody's blaming you for being old, dear, but there's no need to stand right under my feet.'

Alleviation from pain could only be found among his soldiers. Peggy hardly ever went into the garage and there at least he might not feel her presence, nor hear her voice. He asked Nigel to help him up to the garage every morning after breakfast and told him not to come back for him until the afternoon. He wanted to concentrate on the battle of Waterloo. He spent hours poring over maps. Of course he knew every detail of June 18th and the days that led up to it by heart. The Duke of Wellingon was a great man and a great soldier, but for Jack, with his hero-worship of Napoleon, the battle of Waterloo was an occasion of immense pathos. Right up until the morning of June 16th, Napoleon was moving towards victory. The battle was lost, to all intents and purposes, on the night of the 16th and the morning of the 17th when Napoleon had hesitated and failed to move with his customary speed. But could Napoleon really be blamed? The rain, the mud, Ney, Grouchy, fate – they were all equally responsible.

Jack wanted his layout of Waterloo to be better than anything he had made before. Over the months he had prepared most of his soldiers but the terrain was far from ready and he would need time to prepare the buildings – the white farmhouse of La Haye Sainte, Papelotte Farm, and so forth. He had his work cut out, and it absorbed him.

Josephine did not come home again for over a month, but she did write several times. Jack also heard from Daphne Brown to whom he had written about Peggy's death. Daphne was planning to spend a few days in Torquay at the end of August, staying with a sister-in-law who lived there. Nothing, she said, would give her more pleasure than to break her journey at Exeter and to stay the night at Chadcombe before taking the train on to Torquay. Jack wrote back to say that nothing could give him more pleasure than to see Daphne. He hoped she wouldn't mind sleeping in Josephine's room. It was quite a nice little room really.

It occurred to Jack that he might be able to finish Waterloo by the time Daphne arrived. He was sure that she would be interested to see it and the prospect of her arrival gave him an added spur. He wasn't quite sure whether he had worked out the lie of the land quite satisfactorily yet. He thought he would need a few more layers of *papier mâché* before he could be satisfied with the ridge at Mont-St-Jean. Of course, there could be no doubt about it, Wellington's choice of battleground was nothing short of inspired and Jack wanted to reproduce it as accurately as possible.

Every day Jack worked away and his absorption in his subject helped to dull the pain of his loss. Suzanne was worried about him. He never ate any lunch and had grown remarkably thin. He looked older than his seventy-five years.

By the time Daphne was due to arrive, the battlefield was ready. A miniscule Iron Duke mounted on a chestnut thoroughbred had taken up his position under a tiny elm tree on the crossroads at Mont-Saint-Jean. The allied army was deployed along the ridge, the infantry and artillery in front, the cavalry behind, all silently waiting for the battle to begin. The guards occupied the outlying farm of Hougoumont and the King's German Legion were in place at La Haye Sainte. To the east lay the Paris Wood with the Prussian army ready to break through and join the fray, and facing the allies, awaiting defeat, lay the French. D'Erlon's corps was ready to take La Haye Sainte, and there were the dragoons, the cuirassiers and the

Imperial Guard bringing up the rear, each little painted man representing so many hundreds more. Expectant of victory, the great Emperor himself sat confidently on his white horse ready to advance to his forward position at La Belle Alliance.

Jack proudly surveyed his armies, his left hand resting on a stick, his right hand tucked into the front of his jacket. They were beautiful indeed. And this battlefield was a triumph. Nigel and Suzanne who came to admire it were quite bowled over by the splendour of it all.

Daphne was due to arrive late the following afternoon. Nigel would meet her at the station if Jack would look after the shop. Suzanne had promised to make an especially nice supper.

'Last time Daphne came it was before her husband died,' said Jack. 'They came together. Peggy cooked us a lovely lunch. I remember we had a chicken and carrots in white sauce – and roast potatoes. Mustn't forget the roast potatoes. It was good of Peggy. Very good, because you see, she didn't care for cooking. But she gave us a lovely lunch all the same – and very kind of her it was too.'

'Don't worry,' said Suzanne, 'I'll see to it that we have something special. How about a nice piece of beef and an apple pie?'

Jack thought that that sounded lovely, but he was worried about the drink. Could Suzanne get some sherry? A dry one and a medium one, he thought. It was better to be able to offer a choice. Suzanne assured him that she would do just that, although she wondered how on earth she was going to carry it all back on the bus.

Jack also wanted a bottle of wine. He didn't want to be a nuisance, but could she go to Baillie Vintners in her lunch hour? They would advise her on a good claret. In his young days he had often enjoyed a bottle of Lynch-Bages or a Beychevelle. He had no idea what either of those would cost nowadays. He dreaded to think, but he would like something a little special. After all Daphne was coming a long way and he didn't see her very often.

The next day Jack busied himself preparing for Daphne's arrival. There was not much in the garden at this time of year but there were a few dahlias – pretty pompon dahlias – which

Nigel had planted out in April. Jack picked a bunch and arranged some in a vase in the sitting room and a few in a little jug which he asked Mrs Chedzoy to carry up to Daphne's room. Jack didn't like to tackle the stairs more often than he had to. Then he went to the corner cupboard in the sitting room and took out the best cut glass. He polished the sherry glasses carefully before arranging them neatly on a tray.

By the time Daphne arrived with Nigel everything was in order and the sitting room looked as neat as a pin.

Daphne was older than Jack but she didn't look it, he thought. She was upright and brisk and pretty, with a girlish voice and a tinkling laugh. Her softly waved white hair was still quite thick and her mauve cardigan brought out the blue of her eyes. Jack was delighted to see her. It quite took him out of himself.

When Suzanne came in from work she and Nigel sat and had a glass of sherry with Jack and Daphne. Then Suzanne went to the kitchen to prepare the supper while Nigel disappeared to do something in the shop.

Daphne and Jack sat over their sherry, talking about this and that. They discussed the weather, the miners' strike and the state of the world. Neither of them would have liked to be young now – the world had become too nasty a place what with all the violence, unemployment, sexual licence and so forth. They found themselves agreeing about almost everything.

After an excellent supper – Suzanne had managed to find some beautiful wine, the price of which appalled Jack – Nigel and Suzanne retired to an early bed. Jack and Daphne sat up talking until late into the night. Their conversation became more personal as Jack told Daphne about his soldiers which he would show her in the morning, about Josephine and how he missed her, about the problems of living with his stepson and daughter-in-law. He was worried about being in their way although he had to admit that they were always very kind to him. He spoke of Bobby and of Peggy, of his guilt at Peggy's death and of the future. What remained of the future for him? Daphne listened to it all with warmth and understanding.

He must, he thought next morning, have been a bit tiddly. It wasn't like him to talk about himself in that way. Indeed he

168

must have been tiddly to have asked Daphne to marry him. What damned impertinence! But in the clear light of morning he could still see exactly how it had happened. There had been Daphne, pretty, kind and gentle, humorous and intelligent, looking like a much older Bobby – what could be more suitable than that the two of them should end their days together? They shared the same understanding of the world and neither of them expected anything more from it.

Daphne, of course, had refused. She laughed her girlish laugh. The last thing she had expected at her age was a proposal of marriage, but she was flattered and deeply touched. She did not think that such an undertaking would be wise at this stage. She treasured Jack's friendship and hoped that shortly he would be able to come and stay with her again, but she felt that he was suffering from the effects of Peggy's recent death. Bereavement did strange things to one. It had taken her a long time to adjust herself to being alone after Maurice died. Perhaps she had not yet adjusted herself completely. She knew that as time passed things would fall into perspective for Jack and he would begin to feel differently. In the meantime she urged him to try not to feel guilty. She was sure that he had no reason for guilt.

When Daphne came down in the morning, Suzanne had already left for work and Nigel had gone to open the shop. Jack was making toast and had the water boiling ready for Daphne's egg.

As she came into the kitchen Jack felt bound to apologise for his behaviour the evening before.

'Dear Jack,' said Daphne, 'please don't apologise. You have nothing to apologise for,' and patted him on the arm. 'Now what I am really looking forward to this morning is the battle of Waterloo!'

When Daphne had finished admiring Waterloo, it was time for Nigel to drive her to the station. She wished Jack a fond goodbye and begged him to return the visit soon. As he waved her off, he felt a strange sense of loss.

He went into the sitting room and picked up his book. He sat down and began to read, but his mind kept wandering to Peggy and Daphne and back again to Peggy.

That afternoon he asked Nigel to help him up the garden to the garage. He might find some peace among his soldiers. When Nigel had left him, he sat down and surveyed the battlefield. It was a pity he had finished it really and that there was nothing left that he could do to improve it. What next? he thought, what next? – and sighed.

Chapter XVIII

By the autumn Nigel and Suzanne were beginning to worry about Jack. It was not really that he was in the way nor that he was demanding or difficult to look after. It was just that they were beginning to feel that they needed more room. Nigel wanted to expand the shop and had applied for a licence to sell wines and spirits and Suzanne had discovered to her delight that she was pregnant.

Ever since Peggy died Suzanne had been thinking that it would be a good idea for her and Nigel to change rooms with Jack. Jack's room was much bigger than theirs, and altogether more suitable for a couple, but Nigel had been hesitant. Jack had always been decent to Nigel and Nigel felt that it was a bit soon to start making changes.

Then there was the problem of the ownership of the shop. At first it had been presumed that Peggy had died intestate in which case Jack would have a life interest in the shop and an outright claim to everything else, but shortly after Peggy died Nigel received a letter from a solicitor in Exeter which amazed him by informing him that his mother had made a will leaving her property equally divided between himself and Josephine. She had, as it turned out, consulted the solicitor concerning her right to sell the shop over Jack's head and at the time the solicitor persuaded Peggy to make a will. This all happened shortly after Jack's stroke and Peggy, determined not to listen to reason, had refused to consider the possibility of Jack's outliving her and had left everything to her children.

At first Nigel thought that he could not tell Jack about the will. After all, what difference would it make? It was clear that he and Suzanne could hardly turn the old boy out into the cold. He wondered whether or not he should even tell Josephine, but soon discovered that this had been done for him by Peggy's solicitor.

Josephine initially agreed to do nothing. She did not want half a shop. But as she sat in Manchester brooding about her future and wondering about her increasingly difficult relationship with Russell, it occurred to her that although she had no need of half a shop, the money would come in nicely. She wrote to Nigel suggesting that he buy her out. Nigel was not displeased by the idea. He liked the thought of entirely owning his small business and he had the little bit of money left him by his grandmother. Besides, it seemed to him that Josephine's share would not be all that large since he could reasonably expect to claim the goodwill for his own.

Inevitably Josephine was displeased. She was not going to let that creepy Nigel get away with anything. A great quarrel began and numerous visits to solicitors ensued. Naturally Jack could not be kept in the dark, but when he learned what was going on, he was surprisingly resigned about it all. Nigel assured him that it would make no difference to Jack as he would always be welcome to make his home with Suzanne and himself.

Jack had slowed down dreadfully in the last few months and although he talked a great deal about his soldiers and what he would do with them next, he rarely seemed to be able to make it to the garage. If he did go there, Nigel was loath to leave him for long. For one thing there was no lavatory. The stairs in the house had also become a problem. It took Jack an age to climb them at night or to come down them in the morning. He hardly ever went to the pub any more either although he just managed to get down to the church on Remembrance Sunday. As often as not he even sent Nigel on his behalf to the travelling library which, after all, stopped only a couple of hundred yards away from the post office.

'Don't you think,' said Suzanne to Nigel in bed one night, 'that Jack would probably be better off in an old people's home?'

'A home?' Nigel was amazed. The idea had never even crossed his mind. 'You don't put people in homes. Not unless they're unbearable people like my mother.'

'But,' Suzanne explained, 'it wouldn't be a question of

172

"putting" him in a home. If we discuss it with him nicely he'll be bound to see that it's a good idea.'

'How can you possibly think that?' Nigel asked, turning over and settling into a comfortable position ready to go to sleep.

'Well, it's obvious. He wouldn't have the problem of the stairs. He'd have people of his own age to mix with and of course we would go and see him and bring him out for the day every so often. I'm sure he'd be much happier.'

Nigel refused to discuss the matter any further. He was tired and wanted to go to sleep. But the seed was sown.

A few days later, Suzanne wanted to ask a friend from work and her husband round for supper.

'What are we going to do about Jack?' Suzanne asked.

'What do you mean – what are we going to do about Jack? Nothing, of course.'

'Well, when Chris and Beverley come round. He won't want to see them.'

'I can't think why not,' said Nigel. 'They're perfectly nice people.'

'Well, it'll be embarrassing for him, won't it?' said Suzanne.

'I can't think why.'

'Of course it will – what with me and Beverley both being pregnant.'

'I can't quite see what that has to do with it.'

Nigel was furious with Suzanne when she told him she was pregnant. He told her that it must be perfectly clear that this was to be a once-off affair. There were to be no more babies. And fancy getting pregnant at a time like this, when he had the whole problem of Josephine and the shop on his hands. He had not yet accustomed himself to the fact and on the whole he preferred not to discuss the matter. He had a lurking, childish feeling that if the problem were not mentioned, it might go away.

'Well,' Suzanne went on determinedly, 'Beverley and I might want to discuss our symptoms.'

Nigel felt momentarily sick. Nobody, he said, would want to hear about Beverley's or Suzanne's symptoms.

In the event no one discussed their symptoms and Jack retired to bed immediately after supper, leaving the young

173

people to enjoy themselves. Nigel thought that the evening had gone off very well.

Suzanne's next line of attack was not much different. Jack, she said, would hardly welcome the arrival of a baby in the post office. He had been ever so friendly when Suzanne told him about it and had warmly congratulated her and Nigel. But when you came to think about it, it was obvious that, at his age, Jack would only be aggravated by the presence of a baby. He wasn't a young man any more and what old people needed more than anything else was a little peace and quiet. Well he wasn't likely to get much peace and quiet in the post office once the baby was born. After all it would be crying all night and most of the day too.

Nigel winced at the thought of the baby crying all night and most of the day. Suzanne had announced that it was to sleep in their bedroom and it occurred to him that it would be he, not Jack, who would be looking for peace and quiet.

At the beginning of November Jack was unwell. He retired to bed for a few days with 'flu. He felt pretty sorry for himself, but he didn't complain. Nigel and Suzanne and Mrs Chedzoy waited on him in turns and it bothered him to think of the trouble he was causing.

One evening when he was still in bed, and as Nigel and Suzanne sat watching the television, Suzanne returned to the attack. This time more directly.

Nobody could say that Suzanne was unkind. So long as Jack lived with them, she would look after him. But she was beginning to have had enough. She was pregnant and still working and yet when she came home in the evening she was expected to trail up and down stairs with trays for Jack. It was too much. And she didn't blame Jack either. He was a nice old boy and it wasn't his fault that he was old and ill. But he wasn't even Nigel's father. Didn't Nigel realise that he had no responsibility for Jack? Josephine was the one who ought to be looking after him. He was her father and she was supposed to be so fond of him, and did she ever come back and see him? Oh no. Not if she could help it. Josephine was too busy thinking about herself. And if Josephine wasn't prepared to look after Jack, why should she and Nigel? Mind you, if it were Peggy

174

upstairs with 'flu, Suzanne wouldn't so much as take her a cup of tea. She asked herself how they had all put up with that woman for so long. As for Jack, it was perfectly obvious that he would be happier in an old people's home. She was surprised that Nigel couldn't see it.

Nigel thought that Suzanne was being selfish, but he was beginning to see that she had a point. In any case Suzanne was not selfish in the way that Peggy had been selfish. She respected Jack's feelings to the extent that she never ever complained in front of him. It was quite true that she was always prepared to make him cups of tea and run errands for him in Exeter. She even did his washing and ironing if Mrs Chedzoy didn't have time.

But Nigel was not convinced that Jack would be happy in an old people's home. If he could convince himself of that, he would have no hesitation in bringing the matter up with Jack. Nigel's conscience pricked him. He could not forget that the post office had been bought with Jack's money and that it was by a most unlikely chance that Peggy had died first and by an even more unlikely chance that she had made a will which cut her husband out.

Suzanne couldn't see that that made any difference. If Jack had died first, the property would still have come to Nigel and Josephine on their mother's death.

'Probably not,' said Nigel 'She would have sold the shop over our heads and turned us out. Then she would most likely have spent all the money and died penniless.'

Suzanne could see no point in dwelling on what had not happened.

Nigel stretched and stood up.

'Bedtime,' he said. 'Neither of us is paying any attention to the television, I'll turn it off.'

Suzanne was knitting a blanket for the baby. She wanted to finish her row.

It would be nice, Nigel thought as he turned to leave the room, to have the house to themselves. When Suzanne came up to bed he said:

'I'll think about it. But please don't rush things, and don't say anything to Jack. We can't make any decision until we've

175

spoken to Josephine. After all, as you rightly point out, he is her father. We'll discuss it with her when she next comes home.'

Nigel was fully aware that no discussion he was ever likely to have with Josephine could be expected to run smoothly. She automatically opposed him whenever she had the opportunity. It was a pity that he could no longer hold the robbery from the till over her. But then she had had something to hold over him in those days, too. Ah well, he would have to tread carefully.

Josephine didn't come home again until the end of November. She shouldn't really have come then because it meant missing classes, but she had quarrelled with Russell and wanted to get away for a few days. She would have to pretend to have been ill. Besides she remembered how she had promised herself that she would go home to see her father once a month after Peggy died. Peggy had died at the end of June and apart from the funeral, she had only been home once. Her poor old father must be fed up living with Nigel and Suzanne. She thought he sounded quite sad from his letters, and she knew she ought to go and see him. Somehow when she was away from home she didn't think about him much – and then the weeks went by so quickly.

When Josephine arrived home, Jack was thrilled to see her, but she was shocked to find how her father had aged over the last few months. More than that, she was shocked at how deferential and apologetic – almost servile – he had become towards that nasty Nigel and fat Suzanne. Josephine hated the idea that Nigel and Suzanne were now more or less in charge of her father and that her father was dependent on them – and not only dependent on them but fond of them. Nigel had no claim on her father's affections.

She planned to stay at home for three days. By the end of the first twenty-four hours she had already decided that something must be done about the situation. She must talk to that selfish Nigel.

Suzanne was irritated by Josephine. The house was too crowded with her around. As it was the sitting room had become uninhabitable since Jack had brought some of his campaign maps and soldiers into it. The sooner he was settled

176

in a nice home, the better it would be for everyone. But she had promised Nigel to say nothing, and he was biding his time. You had to pick your moment with Josephine.

After breakfast on her second day at home, Josephine followed Nigel into the shop. Jack was in the sitting room reading the newspaper.

'Look here, Nigel, I want to speak to you,' said Josephine. 'I think we ought to do something about my father. He's not happy here, you know. I think he would be much happier in a home for old people.'

Nigel couldn't believe his ears. It was too good to be true. Jack actually wanted to go.

'Are you sure?' he asked. But he had to wait for an answer as a customer had just come into the shop.

Josephine leaned against the wall and stared rudely as Nigel fetched bacon and fruit and corned beef and piled them neatly on the counter. It occurred to her that with Jack out of the post office, the way would be clear for her solicitor to go for Nigel. She didn't really want to involve her father in the whole thing. How dare Nigel think that he could cheat her out of her rightful share!

When Nigel's customer had packed her shopping carefully into her basket and left the shop with a cheery 'goodbye', he turned back to Josephine. He would have to be careful. He didn't want to put Josephine's back up.

'Are you sure your father's not happy here?' he asked again.

'Of course he isn't,' snapped Josephine. 'How could he be? He can hardly walk upstairs, he can't get to the garage and in a minute there'll be a baby bawling at him all day. Use your imagination. What's more,' she added rudely, 'he needs to be with people who can look after him properly.'

That night, in their bedroom, Nigel told Suzanne about his conversation with Josephine. Suzanne was so relieved. It was wonderful to know that they would be doing the best thing for Jack. They decided not to mention the matter to him until they had found somewhere nice for him to go. With the little bit of money he had he could probably afford a modest private home.

Josephine agreed with Nigel's and Suzanne's plan. She told them to look around for somewhere locally, but not to come to

177

any decisions until they had asked her. She didn't want her father put away in any old place. She would come back herself during the Christmas holidays and give her approval. Then she could probably help Jack to move. He would want to take a few things. She had heard that you could take your own furniture to some of these homes.

In a million years Jack had not thought it would come to this. To think that only a few weeks ago he was contemplating marriage, and now his only option was an old people's home.

When they told him, he was quite simply shocked. Utterly flabbergasted. What had made them think that he was unhappy? He was considerably happier in the post office than he would ever be in an old people's home. And to think that Josephine and Nigel had plotted it all behind his back. Wasn't there something in Shakespeare about having an ungrateful child? Sharper than a serpent's tooth . . . ? He even remembered taking Josephine to see *King Lear* years ago at the Northcote Theatre.

He stared uncomprehendingly at their three faces as they stood in a threatening row in front of him.

'It's a lovely place we've found,' said Suzanne. 'I'm sure you'll like it.'

'You'll be much happier there,' said Josephine.

'It's not that we don't want you,' said Nigel.

Jack said nothing. He just thought back over his life. It had been a good life on the whole. It had had its ups and downs, but he had seen the world, loved, even been loved, he had developed absorbing interests – interests in which he had been able to lose himself and which had prevented him from ever being lonely – and now this. A genteel old people's home on the outskirts of Exeter with room for a few of his own possessions!

Still he said nothing and still they stood in front of him mouthing inane platitudes.

There was nothing for him to say. He was far too proud to beg to remain where he was clearly not wanted. Of course he had been idiotic. How could he have expected Nigel – who was not even his son – and Suzanne to want an old man living with them, particularly now that they were going to have a baby.

But he would never understand Josephine. What on earth, he wondered, had persuaded her to fall in with them? There was nothing for it but to accept defeat, as his great hero, Napoleon, had been forced to do. Those three insignificant people in front of him represented the allied powers, and he must capitulate. He wondered what would have happened if Peggy had not written that will? Or if Blücher hadn't arrived on time, or if Grouchy hadn't taken the wrong road, or if it hadn't rained . . . .

They told him that they would have him settled in by Christmas. Wouldn't that be nice? And of course they would come over on Christmas Day and take him out for lunch. That would be something to look forward to. In the meantime they would help him pack up his things.

The bitterest blow came when they told him that he would not be able to take his soldiers. They had discussed the possibility with the matron but there was clearly no room for them, and, besides, the domestic staff would complain.

Jack glanced out of the window. It was beginning to snow.

'By the time the Grand Army crossed the Nieman,' he said, 'only 30,000 of the original 600,000 soldiers were still alive.'

'Yes,' said Suzanne brightly, 'it was a grand army. The grandest army I've ever seen, with the sweetest little soldiers.'

'It was at exactly this time of year,' said Jack. 'The temperature at Smolensk was minus thirty degrees centigrade.'

'Oh dear,' said Suzanne. 'I hope you're not cold. We don't want you to catch cold just now.'

Nigel and Suzanne drove Jack to his new home. Josephine sat next to her father in the back. No one spoke much.

High laurel hedges lined the drive that led to the house. As they drove between them, Jack was strangely reminded of the Corinth Canal – how many many years seemed to have passed since that cruise. And of course the Corinth Canal opened into the bright, rich Aegean Sea, whereas this gloomy avenue opened on something quite different. He had seen the name painted on a board as they swept in through the gate. *Saint Helena's Residential Home for the Elderly*. That was quite

179

funny, he thought. Really quite funny. And I can put up with this black basalt rock, he thought, this extinct volcano, this little island, but, without my soldiers, I shall be dreadfully lonely.